Narragansett Justice

ROBERT B. STONE

Narragansett Justice © 2025 Robert B. Stone.

First Stillwater River Publications Edition

Library of Congress Control Number: 2025912949
ISBN: 978-1-965733-75-2
12345678910
Written by Robert B. Stone.
Published by Stillwater River Publications, West Warwick, RI, USA.

Publisher's Cataloging-in-Publication
(Provided by Cassidy Cataloguing Services, Inc.)

Names: Stone, Robert B. (Robert Bailey), author.
Title: Narragansett justice / Robert B. Stone.
Description: First Stillwater River Publications edition. | West Warwick, RI, USA : Stillwater River Publications, [2025]
Identifiers: LCCN: 2025912949 | ISBN: 9781965733752 (paperback)
Subjects: LCSH: Narragansett Indians--History--17th century--Fiction. | Indians of North America--History-- Colonial period, ca. 1600-1775--Fiction. | Pioneers--New England--History--17th century--Fiction. | British--New England--History--17th century--Fiction. | Land settlement--New England--History-- 17th century--Fiction. | New England--History--Colonial period, ca. 1600-1775--Fiction. | LCGFT: Historical fiction.
Classification: LCC: PS3619.T675 N37 2025 | DDC: 813/.6--dc23

For my family,

My friends,

And those who will read and enjoy

ACKNOWLEDGEMENTS

THIS BOOK WOULD LIKELY NOT HAVE BEEN COMPLETED without the assistance of a very few people whose expertise and patient contribution to the project became critical to the story's completion. The story itself came from a dream. However, the manner in which the book developed can be attributed in great part to two people I acknowledge here.

Albert Dercole, a friend for several years, has been fascinated by the language of the Narragansett people for over thirty year. He has been studying Southern New England Algonquin (SNEA) and compiling words from sources such as historic language lists, court documents, deeds, and diaries to such an extent that he was invited to be a part of the Language Reclamation Team at the Mashantucket Pequot Tribal Museum working under a federal grant.

Through Mr. Dercole, I met Rashad Young who is Director of the Language Department at the Mashantucket Pequot Museum. Mr. Young was born in Providence. His mother is Pequot and Narragansett, and his father is Narragansett and Pokanoket. He spent his childhood in Ledyard, Connecticut just off the Mashantucket Pequot Reservation which allowed him to have cultural values and traditions close at hand. After obtaining his college degree in Computer Science and holding several positions in business, he was drawn back to his tribe and its culture and joined the language program of which he is now director.

The SNEA language is not without some disagreement even among the experts. I have confidence that we have arrived at the most readable and accurate representation of the language possible.

I must recognize the contribution of my perennial proofreader Margaret (Maggie) Skenyon. Her attention to details of syntax, punctuation, and spelling makes my writing better. I must also recognize the contribution of my wife, Angela. It is she who slogs through the early drafts of the story and corrects many of the mistakes in continuity and flow of the reading.

As a final acknowledgement, it was at the suggestion of Albert Dercole that footnotes be used to allow the reader quick reference to SNEA words used in the story. This keeps the reader "in the story" without requiring them to turn to a reference glossary or listing elsewhere in the book to understand the word and lose the continuity of the story.

To all of the above, I owe my gratitude.

PREFACE

THIS IS A STORY THAT ORIGINATED IN A DREAM AS ALL OF my stories do. It is a murder/mystery set in the time just prior to King Philip's War (1675-1676) in which the woodland tribes of New England fought with the colonist of Massachusetts, Connecticut and Rhode Island. It was a time when tensions were increasing between the Indigenous Peoples and the colonists. The characterizations and suspicions of both sides were near a breaking point. Most of the colonists saw the natives as murderous savages. But a small number sought friendship and understanding. This is the story of one such friendship.

ONE

SPRING HAD COME. THE MORNING AIR NOW HELD THE sweet expectation of new growth. You could feel it in the warming rays of the rising sun. The night still held the coolness of winter, and a blanket kept the chill from one sleeping, but you could tell winter had lost its hold. The ice no longer piled up against the shore and was gone from the coves, and wind-driven spray no longer coated the marsh grass along the shore with heavy ice crystals. Now, a lighter morning dew rapidly lost its glitter as the sun of late spring climbed above the horizon. There was the promise of a good year in this, the twelfth summer of a young brave's life. Nupanawôquhsak (Five Red Foxes) wiped sleep from his eyes and pulled his doeskin blanket just a bit higher as sunlight began to warm the east side of his family's bark longhouse.

It had been a harsh winter. The hunting had been sparse, and the game had gone deeper into the woods. Smaller game had stayed hidden in their burrows and lairs. Ice had clogged the shore and frozen much of the coves making fishing more difficult. The stored corn and nuts harvested last fall were running a bit lower than usual. The stews of grasses, roots, corn, shellfish, and nuts Wôquhsak's (Red Foxes') mother cooked on the fire were hearty and warming, but it was no substitute for the rich aroma of meat. It had been the smell of such a stew that had awakened Wôquhsak (Red Foxes) now.

3

He rolled back his hide covers and slid into his deerskin leggings. He pulled on his well-worn mahkusunash[1] on his feet and strode past his mother drawing the aroma of her cooking deep into his nose. He was heading for the doorway of the quneekamug[2] to wash his face with what he knew would be bracingly chilly water. It was much earlier than they normally would have moved to the summer campsite nearer the great bay, and the hastily constructed bark longhouse provided better shelter until the cattails grew large enough to construct the summer putukuhkun[3] made of woven mats of reeds and cattails. The ability to fish and gather crabs and shellfish would add needed protein to their diet.

As he went through the doorway, his mother looked after him admiring her son. He had grown tall over the winter, taller than most people his age. His frame was sturdy but did not betray the full strength of his young muscles. His waist was tight and defined and he walked with a confident stride on strong legs. His straight hair fell beyond his shoulders and was as black as a raven's wing. She was proud of him. He would be a good husband some day for some lucky mutumwu-hsuhs[4] and warrior and tribal leader. But she secretly hoped to herself that it might still be just a few more years away.

As soon as Wôquhsak stepped from the longhouse, the cool morning air of the day greeted him. He walked to the side of the structure where the skin buckets were kept. He took a bucket and walked toward the freshwater spring that fed the small stream running near the edge of the clan's summer encampment. Kneeling at the edge of the stream just below the spring, Wôquhsak dipped the bucket into the cold, clear water. The icy water ran over his hand. He knew the water would be cold, but his morning ritual required him to wash his upper body no matter how cold the water might be. With a deep breath, he plunged

---

[1] Moccasins
[2] Two fire longhouse
[3] Round summer shelter of cattail mats
[4] Woman. The term "squaw" is a loan word adapted into American English from Algonquin

4

his hands into the bucket and tossed the water on his face and chest trying to hold back the screech he wanted so badly to let out. By the third toss of water, Wôquhsak could no longer feel the coolness of the morning air from the cold of the water. He tipped what liquid was left in the bucket onto the ground and walked quickly back to his family's longhouse. Putting the bucket back near the others by the side of the house, he crossed his arms over his chest and sprinted back inside the longhouse to the warmth of the fire and for some good, warm stew.

Wôquhsak's mother, Upeeshâwônkoon (Snow Flower), handed him a steaming wooden bowl and bone spoon as he approached. Already seated by the fire was Wôquhsak's younger cousin, Mushqeenupeeash (Red Waters). They were close in age, but Mushqeenupeeash was smaller in stature and had a personality that was lively and mischievous. He complimented Wôquhsak's personality perfectly. As Wôquhsak sat at the fire next to his cousin, feeling the warmth of the stew in his belly, Mushqeenupeeash poked him with his elbow almost causing him to spill his steaming bowl while pretending to be deeply concentrating on his own bowl of stew. Mushqeenupeeash broke into a broad smile and laughed as Wôquhsak momentarily feigned anger and then laughed as well. Wôquhsak's mother looked at them sitting before the fire, laughing together, and smiled. They were growing up and she was proud of them. What she did not know was the surprise these two young men had been planning through the dreariness of the winter months. Little did they realize the frightening adventure that would occupy their young lives and the lives of those they loved for much of the next season.

As they sat before the fire, finishing the last of the stew lovingly prepared by Wôquhsak's mother, the two boys shared knowing smiles as they whispered about their plans for the day. It was a day for which they had carefully prepared all through the winter. The pelts of beaver, otter, and fox they had secretly prepared over the preceding months had been carefully stacked outside the longhouse the night before under protective coverings, along with the four fathoms of wampum they had meticulously fashioned during the frigid winter. Arrangements had been made for the use of one of the heavier muhshoon[5] canoes of the clan. All had been done in utmost secrecy.

Wôquhsak's father Nuhshwanum Nâhneepawuhshat (Three Dogs Moon) had left three suns earlier to hunt for the family. He could be gone as long as ten moons to find game. Game was moving farther away as settlers began building homes in the wilderness of Narragansett lands. But he had approved of the plan his son had formed before he left. His father knew Wôquhsak was young to be conducting such a plan and yet, he would need to take on this responsibility eventually. He also knew his son wanted to do his part for the family.

Mushqeenupeeash had become a member of the family when his father had died two years ago from the white man's pox. His mother, sister to Wôquhsak's mother, had survived, but showed many scars on her face and arms from the illness she had also experienced. Mushqeenupeeash's father had traded that fall two years before with a wôpusu[6] he did not know for blankets to keep his family warm when the harsh winter weather set in. Many in this small clan of ten families suspected the white man's blankets were the source of the disease. The blankets were burned after the death of Mushqeenupeeash's father, and the Elders of the clan warned others not to trade for any kind of fabric and stay away from blankets.

Wôquhsak had no intentions of trading for anything other than what he knew his mother needed and wanted. The large iron cooking kettle pot she possessed was her pride and joy, and after ten years of hard, daily use, it was a bit dented, and the metal had worn thin. It was still the envy of the clan even in its present condition. A new cast-iron pot, like the one she had used that very morning to prepare their breakfast stew, would be his contribution to the family. His father would hunt for their food, and he would provide the means for cooking it.

---

[5] Dugout canoe- usually white pine for coastal
[6] White Man

Finished eating, the two boys left the fire and quickly finished dressing. As they prepared to leave the longhouse, each boy gave Wôquhsak's mother a hug and acknowledged the caution she gave them every morning to have a good day and to be careful. The morning sun was quickly warming the air as Wôquhsak and Mushqeenupeeash stepped into the opening in front of the longhouse. If the waters were calm, this would be the day. They walked through the summer camp to the shore of the great pootupâq[7] that the white men called Narragansett after the natives on the west shore of the great bay and watched the water for a few moments. This had been the chosen location for the clan's summer camp for as long as Wôquhsak could remember and long before that. Sheltered by a spit of land running north and a small promontory to the east and cliffs to the south, the camp was protected from east winds and the heavier waves that storms could whip up in the bay. But this day's conditions looked perfect. The wind was light; the waves were small, and the tide was running into the bay. They looked at each other and nodded in agreement: yes, everything was favorable for the trip up the bay this day.

The two boys sprinted back through camp to the side of the long-house where their cache of pelts and wampum were hidden in a woven basket. They quietly removed the protective coverings of hides, leaving only the large bearskin, and retrieved the hidden bundles of pelts and the bag of wampum. Walking away from the side of the house, carrying the basket covered by the larger bearskin between them, the young boys took a route back to the shore so they would not be seen by anyone inside their longhouse. They slowly walked to the shore where the clan's canoes were pulled up on the sand and picked one of the muhshoon[8] that was about five spans in length and sturdy enough for their trip to the trading posts to the north. At about twelve feet in length, the dugout allowed plenty of room for them to store their basket and paddle comfortably on their trip. With their pelts and wampum

---

[7] Bay, or large body of water
[8] Dugout Canoe – usually white pine for coastal

stowed aboard in the basket covered with a bearskin and paddles in hand, the two boys pushed their craft into the calm, protected waters of the shore and stepped aboard. A few deft strokes with their wutahôq[9] swung the canoe away from the shallows of the shore and put it on a course north along the shoreline.

As they cleared the north point of the small peninsula that protected their summer camp from the larger waters of pootupâq[10], the current of the incoming tide pushed them along, as did a following wind. It was pleasant paddling leisurely just offshore with the sun warming their skin. The muhshoon[11] skimmed along as the paddles dipped into the calm water under the powerful strokes of the two youngsters. The shoreline was devoid of trees in several spots where different clans of ununowak[12] had summer camps. Wherever fresh water was near at hand from the many streams and springs along the shore, this was where the people had settled during the warm summer months for centuries. The trees had been cut down to allow for gardens to be planted. They passed a couple of summer campsites that were just being established by clans that had come to the shore a little later than their clan but not late for the season. Large plots of corn, beans, and squash were already planted. So far, it was one of those days where everything seemed at peace and memorable.

As the young braves paddled along the shoreline, Wôquhsak thought about the two trips he had previously made to the trading posts with his father. It was his experience on those trips that had given him the confidence to propose this plan to his father. He knew he was younger than most of those who went to trade with the wôpusuwak[13]. He knew bargaining for a good trade would not be easy, especially when he would be thought to be too young by the white men to know how to go about getting a decent price. But he had watched intently

---

[9] Canoe paddles
[10] Bay, or large body of water
[11] See note 7
[12] Our People – the Narragansett
[13] White Men

when his father had bartered on those two trips, and he knew what signs to look for from the trader agent. He knew to be stoic in appearance and be sure he understood what the trader said no matter how long it might take to gain that understanding. After all, not speaking a common language was a barrier and sometimes signs were not understood or misunderstood.

They had been paddling with their flat-bladed wutahôq[14] for more than two hours and were approaching the large cove where the mamahchâyukamuq (trading posts) of the wôpusuwak[15] were located on the north shore of the cove behind a small island. These trading posts had replaced the trading spot that Wôquhsak had been told had originally been on an island in the bay with wôpusuwak[16] that were called Dutch. There were two trading posts here in this cove, both of which had been established by an agreement with the sachems of the tribe. The one preferred by most of the people belonged to neetôpâwun Williams[17]. Roger Williams was considered a friend. He was liked by the ununuwak[18] and always seemed to try to give them good, fair trades. He wanted to understand their language and culture. He was a friend of the Narragansett.

The other trading post was managed by a man named Wilcox on land granted to a man named Richard Smith. This man, with a name that sounded funny to many of the ununuwak, was not as well liked as neetôpâwun Roger Williams. Wilcox was always hard to bargain with and, to trade with him, one always felt they were overpaying and being exploited. The hope was always that the trading post of Williams would be open. However, it was run only by himself, and he spent much time in the larger wôpusuwak[18] village at the north end of the great bay.

---

[14] Canoe paddles
[15] White Men
[16] Ibid footnote 15
[17] "Our Friend" Williams – Narragansett reference to Roger Williams
[18] Ibid footnote 15

The two paddles worked in unison to swing the muhshoon[19] into the opening of the large cove. Wôquhsak pointed to the sandspit just inside the east side of the cove and told Mushqeenupeeash to turn the canoe toward it. The muhshoon slid easily onto the soft sand of the beach and the two watôquhsak (cousins) turned to face each other.

"I will speak for us," Wôquhsak said to Mushqeenupeeash. "I have been to these trading posts before with my father and know how to barter with them. Do not show any fear and look them straight in the eye. When we are in sight of the buildings, we will raise our paddles over our heads with both hands to show we come in peace and carry no arms."

"But we have our knives, Wôquhsak," Mushqeenupeeash replied.

"We will leave them in the muhshoon[20] when we go to trade," Wôquhsak replied. "We will use our pelts to begin the trade and only use our wampum if we need to."

"One last thing," Wôquhsak said as he gripped Mushqeenupeeash's forearm, "do not enter the trading post. They say ununuwak[21] have gone in and never come out again. We will trade on the ground outside on our bear hide and not on a blanket." Mushqeenupeeash nodded his understanding with eyes widening with fear.

"The ômatamunooak (traders) will see our youth and look for signs that we are afraid," Wôquhsak warned, "We must show we are not afraid."

With those admonishments, the two young braves stepped out of the muhshoon[22] and pushed it back into the water. Carefully settling into the canoe once again, they began paddling around the south side of the island that ran along the northerly side of the cove, where the trading posts were situated. The island would keep them out of sight of the trading posts.

---

[19] Dugout canoe
[20] Dugout Canoe
[21] Our people – the Narragansett
[22] Ibid – footnote 20

Rounding the western tip of the island, the trading post of neetôpâwun Williams[23] came into view. This was the trading post they hoped to see open. Their hearts sank when no activity was to be seen, no flag was flying, and the building itself was shuttered. This was disappointing for Wôquhsak and Mushqeenupeeash to see, but they continued to paddle around the north side of the island and slowly glided past the closed trading post.

A little further east, they could see smoke rising from the chimney of the second trading post. Several dugouts were drawn up on the shore in front of the building and, as they drew closer, they could see several people, both wôpusuwak and ununuwak [24] milling about the trading post.

"Remember what we agreed upon," Wôquhsak cautioned Mushqeenupeeash who sat in the bow of the muhshoon[25]. Mushqeenupeeash nodded in reply.

A few more strokes of their paddles brought them into full view of the people around the building.

"Raise your wutahôq[26] now," Wôquhsak called quietly to Mushqeenupeeash as he raised his own paddle.

Their action was acknowledged from the clearing in front of the trading post by two or three of the wôpusuwak[27] who waived in reply. A few more strokes of their paddles brought the muhshoon[28] gliding into marsh grass that lined the shore a little beyond the front of the building. They landed slightly apart from the other boats pulled up on the shore. Wôquhsak did not want the trader's agents, or members of the other clans who were already there to trade, to know what they held in their boat for trade. In fact, he was not at all happy that there were others there to trade. But they were already there, and he was not

---

[23] "Our Friend" Williams – Narragansett reference to Roger Williams
[24] White Men and our people (the Narragansett)
[25] Dugout canoe
[26] Paddle
[27] White Men
[28] Dugout Canoe

about to give up his chance to impress his cousin Mushqeenupeeash with his skill at bartering with the white trader.

TWO

THE TRADING POST WAS CONSTRUCTED OF ROUGH SPLIT clapboard with a roof of split shingles. The chimney was of rounded native boulders harvested from the cove itself. A small, covered porch at the front gave a bit of shade to the front door and the small window cut into the wall beside the door. A large wooden shutter of exceeding thickness lay back against one side of the window. Its large iron hinges showed the rust of exposure to weather. The visible side of the shutter which would have been on the inside of the building when shut, showed two wooden blocks into which a thick wooden beam might be placed to lock the shutter when closed. The structure looked weather-beaten as if it had stood there for years but it was only a few years old.

The spotty grass in front of the building was only just beginning to turn green, but later in the season it would be worn into patches from the passage of many moccasins and boots as the season of trading progressed. At the water's edge, a short ten- or twelve-foot dock jutted into the cove. This is where boats bringing trade goods would unload and the way most wôpusuwak[29] arrived and left. Only those who lived nearby, and those were few, traveled what the whites called the Pequot Trail running west of the cove and stretching from the settlement of

---

[29] White Men

13

Providence to the north, down the bay, to the Pequot territory further west. Most of those ununuwak[30] who wished to trade with the whites came by water.

As the two young braves approached the building, they could see two other ununuwak[31] in deep barter with white traders. One was trying to purchase fishhooks, lead weights, and twine to fashion a net. He was gesturing with arms waving at the impassive white man who sat on the other side of the blanket spread between them. The second skeetôp[32] was sitting on a separate blanket a few feet away with an array of knives before him. The trader bartering with him was pointing to different blades and holding up fingers to express their prices. The brave sat rubbing his chin with one of his hands with no expression on his face or in his eyes.

As Wôquhsak and Mushqeenupeeash neared the building, they saw the head trader, known as Wilcox, seated on a rocking chair on the porch, his form half hidden by the shade of the overhanging roof. He was dressed in leather breeches smeared with something like grease. His waistcoat was badly wrinkled and missing two silvery buttons, one on his right sleeve, the other on the left side of the row running down his chest. His linen shirt was open at the throat and showed stains from food or tobacco down its front. His boots were covered in muck. He held a long-stemmed tobacco pipe in his discolored teeth. As he saw the young braves approaching, he stirred from his chair and came out from the shade to the edge of the porch. It was then that the young boys caught the odor of tobacco, unwashed body, and rum emanating from this slovenly form.

"Wuneekeesuk, neetôpâwun[33]," Wôquhsak said raising his right hand with an open palm, at the same time stopping as far from Wilcox

---

[30] Our People – the Narragansett
[31] Ibid – footnote 30
[32] Man
[33] "Good day, friend"

as seemed possible and extending his left arm to stop Mushqeenu-peeash from getting any closer.

"And good day to you, young man," Wilcox replied as he removed his pipe from his mouth and swayed slightly as he reached for the rough pole supporting the porch roof. "Come to trade, have ye?" Wilcox asked. Without really understanding what was said, Wôquhsak nodded in agreement.

Wilcox then turned to the open door of the trading post and called in a loud voice to an unseen person within. Wôquhsak could feel Mushqeenupeeash nervously flinch at the sudden outburst from Wilcox. He reached back and steadied Mushqeenupeeash with a touch of his hand.

From inside the building, a person emerged with a blanket folded over his arm. He was more cleanly dressed than Wilcox and smiled at Wôquhsak and Mushqeenupeeash. He pointed to an open area of the grass slightly away from the other negotiations already going on. As soon as Wôquhsak saw the blanket, he backed away from it and pointed to it shaking his head from side to side.

"No blanket," Wôquhsak said emphatically in his broken English. "Skin."

"Say, what," the man replied, "no trade blanket?" Wôquhsak emphatically shook his head from side to side.

Wôquhsak turned to Mushqeenupeeash and told him to bring the large bearskin covering the trade pelt bundles.

"Do not run," he said quickly as he saw Mushqeenupeeash turn to run. "Walk! Do not run!"

Turning back to face the trader agent holding the blanket, Wôquhsak heard Wilcox's voice behind him calling out to the man he stood before.

"Charlie!" Wilcox was saying "Is there a problem?"

"He don't want to trade on a blanket," the agent called back.

As Wôquhsak stood waiting for Mushqeenupeeash to return with the bearskin, he noticed a fellow skeetôp[34] crouched against the end of the trading post building farthest from the porch. He was dressed in ragged clothing, mostly what looked to be cast-offs from the wôpusu-wak[35]. His hair was matted and dirty as no self-respecting brave would ever have permitted. His face was gaunt and drawn as he cowered in a half stupor, leaning against the building as if it supported his frame. He appeared to be oblivious to the activity going on around him.

Just then, Mushqeenupeeash arrived with the large bearskin that had been covering the goods Wôquhsak and he had brought to barter with and spread it on the just greening grass. Wôquhsak turned his attention to trading and dismissed his thoughts of the creature he had observed for now.

It was only then that the agent and his boss Wilcox understood and relaxed. Just then, a voice from inside the trading post called out.

"Wôquhsak? Sun keen[36]?" the voice questioned.

"Awân nah[37]?" Wôquhsak replied. He still could not see who had asked if it was him.

In a moment, a tall man Wôquhsak instantly recognized walked through the door.

"Neetôpâwun[38], Jules," Wôquhsak exclaimed with a smile, turning to greet his friend.

Jules was one of the tallest men Wôquhsak had ever seen. He was fair-haired and powerfully built. He wore an unmistakable cloak and unique hat. It was what made him known to all the indigenous people. The cloak reached nearly to the ground and was the color of very ripe chokeberries or dried blood. But it was the hat for which he was known. The crown was remarkably high, and one side of the long brim

---

[34] Narragansett Man
[35] White Men
[36] "Is that you"
[37] "Who is that"
[38] Friend

was pinned up against the side of the crown showing the manly features of the right side of his face, while the other side drooped down nearly touching his shoulder. It was the same color as his cloak. Under his cloak, Jules wore a fine white shirt and long pants of supple deerskin. The shirt bore lace on the neck and wrists and the material was foreign.

Jules de Vendôme had arrived in Narragansett country four or five years previously. He was not like the other wôpusuwak[39] who frequented the lands of the Narragansett. His dress and speech were different, and he moved with a certain elegance of grace. Perhaps because of this, he was tolerated by most of the wôpusuwak[40] but not fully accepted by many. Some outright despised him for his good relations with the natives.

Friend Jules was known by many of the local clans. He had asked the tribe for permission to build his home along the Pequot Trail south of the trading posts. He had settled in an area close to the Wôquhsak's clan's summer camp and built a small, but serviceable, cabin for himself. His fields surrounded his cabin, and he grew many vegetables in the fertile soil of his land. He was willing to help the natives if food stocks ran low during a harsh winter. He would arrive with grain or meat and share his stocks with the Narragansett. He would sit at their fire, share a meal, and trade stories in his broken speech. He had taken the time to learn their language, at which he had become quite good, and would sit with the elders in counsel when asked. Next to Brother (neechay) Williams, Jules de Vendôme was the best loved and trusted of all the wôpusuwak[41] who had come to the Narragansett country. But what he was best known for was his whistling. He whistled wherever he roamed. Some said he could whistle better than the birds. Although they did not know the name of the melody he most frequently

---

[39] White Men
[40] Ibid footnote 39
[41] White Men

whistled, the Narragansets had heard it so often, they almost knew it by heart. In fact, everyone knew Jules was about when they heard it.

Wôquhsak introduced Mushqeenupeeash as his cousin.

"Why have you come today," friend Jules asked? His speech had a different accent from the Englishmen who had begun settling in Narragansett country. He had once told some of the people that he came from a different place called "New France" and English was not his first language. While this made little difference to the Narragansetts, it apparently made his relationship with some of his fellow wôpusuwak[42] a bit strained.

"I want to buy a new cooking pot for my mother," Wôquhsak said proudly.

"Hmm," Jules mused, "that is a large buy to make."

Mushqeenupeeash broke in, "We have been planning all winter, trapping furs and making wampum." Wôquhsak nodded in agreement.

"Well, in that case, you had best begin your barter," Jules said with a smile.

Nodding in agreement, the boys settled on the bearskin opposite the trading agent and assumed a serious expression.

"Friend Jules," Wôquhsak said looking up at the smiling Frenchman, "will you help us if we need to be understood?" He spoke in his tribal tongue knowing the agent would not understand. Jules nodded agreement, folded his arms across his body, and stood behind the trader, now seated on the bearskin opposite the two youngsters. The trader's agent turned to look up at the Frenchman who only smiled in reply.

The trader turned back to face the boys and opened his arms extending them toward them gesturing as if to say, "what do you want?"

Wôquhsak began by mimicking making a fire. Mushqeenupeeash bent over and blew air out as if helping a flame. Wôquhsak reached to his side and pantomimed placing a pot over the fire. He outlined the

---

[42] White Men

shape of the pot and tried showing he was stirring something in the pot. Neetôpâwun[43] Jules said something to the agent, and it brought an instant look of recognition to his face. The agent held up his hand as if to say 'stop' and uncrossed his legs to stand. He walked into the trading post leaving Wôquhsak and Mushqeenupeeash in anxious anticipation seated on the bearskin.

In a few moments, the agent reappeared carrying a copper pot about half the size Wôquhsak wanted. The trader resumed his seat smiling in anticipation that he had understood the request of his trade partner. The looks on Wôquhsak's and Mushqeenupeeash's faces showed disappointment.

"Isn't this what you wanted?" the trader said in frustration. "This is what we sell most of because pots are expensive." He looked up to Jules, his eyes begging for agreement.

Wôquhsak shook his head and said, "no mushqahkuhq[44]. Mooweeshahkuhq[45]."

Wôquhsak looked to neetôpâwun[46] Jules and said pleadingly," peesh kutanunumaw neenâwun[47]?"

Jules nodded and translated Wôquhsak's request for a large iron pot.

"That's not the normal trading pot," the trader told Jules. "And it'll cost a lot more. You better tell yer young friend that!"

Jules turned to Wôquhsak and told him what the agent had said. As he was doing so, the trader again rose from being seated, grabbing the pot by its handle, and stomped through the trading post door.

"Can you afford it, Wôquhsak?" Jules asked. Wôquhsak thought for a moment and looked at Mushqeenupeeash who had been quietly watching and studying the scene.

---

[43] Friend
[44] Mushqahkuhq – small copper pot, usual in trade
[45] Mooweeshahkuhq – large iron pot
[46] Ibid footnote 43
[47] "Will you help us?"

"You should bring our furs from the muhshoon[48]," he said quietly, "and bring the bag of wampum, but keep it hidden as best you can."

The trader appeared in the doorway of the building carrying an iron cooking pot about the right size. Wilcox stopped him as he stepped through the door, and it was easy to see the concern he had about the pot. It was plain to anyone, whether they understood what was being said or not, Wilcox was telling his agent he had better get top price for what he was carrying.

The trader approached the young boys and placed the iron pot on the bearskin. He resumed his seat and gestured at the pot with his hands, palms up. Wôquhsak nodded his approval and reached for the first bundle of furs Mushqeenupeeash had brought to the edge of the bearskin. Untying the bundle, Wôquhsak displayed the first beaver pelt, stroking it lovingly and showing the underside. There were no holes through the skin and the fur was silky and lustrous. They had done an excellent job of tanning.

The agent took the pelt and held it up to the sunlight. He set it aside and took the next pelt and did the same thing. The third pelt was that of a fox. The bright red hairs were perfectly tanned, and the tail retained its fullness. The agent tried hard to hide his pleasure at seeing such fine work. He knew if his manner betrayed his regard for the work that had gone into these pelts, he would not be able to offer a lower value for them.

The first bundle contained twenty pelts, mostly of beaver with two of fox and one wolf. The agent had seen the second bundle of pelts Mushqeenupeeash had fetched from the muhshoon[49] and motioned for them to be presented to him with the fingers of his right hand. That was when Wôquhsak noticed the agent had only the first two fingers and his thumb on his right hand. Where his ring finger and pinky should have been, were stumps. Wôquhsak wondered if the loss of

---

[48] Dugout canoe
[49] Dugout canoe

these fingers indicated something. Surely, he had not been born with this deformity. Was this trader a thief who had suffered punishment?

It was then that Wôquhsak noticed the form beside the building was watching intently what was occurring while acting as if he was not observing anything. He was dressed somewhat as a Narragansett, yet his clothes were a mixture of wôpusuwak[50] clothing and Narragansett. All were dirty and worn. Wôquhsak thought to himself that was most curious.

The agent went through the second bundle of pelts and nodded his satisfaction with their quality. He turned to Jules who had been quietly observing the transaction and said something Wôquhsak did not understand. Jules stopped smiling and began mildly disagreeing with the agent. Before their voices were raised into an argument, Jules put forward his hand in a motion to silence the agent and he looked at Wôquhsak.

"He says the quality of the furs is excellent," Jules began in his pigeon Narragansett dialect. "But it is not enough." Jules rolled his eyes so the agent would not see. "He is lying. Your skins are some of the finest I have seen here, and he is only looking to get as much from you as he can."

"I can see from his right hand, this man lies," Wôquhsak replied to Jules speaking in his native tongue. "Tell him I know I have given him more in value for this pot than he deserves, but I will give him one thing more if he agrees to one more request."

Jules translated what Wôquhsak had said to the agent. The agent turned to Wôquhsak, and his expression begged the question. Jules was standing behind the seated agent ready to translate.

"I will not argue the steepness of your price for the pot because I know you are charging me too much and I want the pot that badly. I have wampum to trade, as well. How much wampum do you want?"

---

[50] White Men's

Wôquhsak waited while Jules translated for the agent. The agent thought for a moment, rubbing his hand against his chin. He glanced at the two boys and slyly asked of Jules. "Ask them how much wampum they have."

"He is asking how much wampum you have brought with you," Jules relayed. "Do not tell him," Jules warned. "He will want it all and he does not deserve it. Make him tell you how much he wants. It is time for you to take control of the trade," Jules continued giving a small smile.

"Tell him we have enough," Wôquhsak responded. Jules did not tell the trader agent what Wôquhsak said. Instead, he asked him how much more wampum was wanted. In reply, the agent said he wanted five fathoms of wampum. Jules dutifully relayed this to Nepanna.

"Tell him I will give him three and no more," Wôquhsak responded. "And tell him I want a cover for the pot and one other thing in trade." Jules looked a bit confused but did as he was directed. The agent looked at Wôquhsak trying to determine what it was he was seeking.

"What is it he wants besides the cover?" the agent mused aloud. Wôquhsak assumed he knew what was said.

"Tell him I want two long strings of weekânqusuqanash[51] for the three fathoms of wampum."

Jules had never heard this word before and did not know how to translate it. He asked Wôquhsak what it was he sought.

"Shukanees[52]," he replied and went on to explain how it appeared. "They are sweet rocks on a string." Jules understood and told the agent. Wôquhsak wanted two long strings of rock candy. The agent gave out a loud laugh and nodded in agreement. He stood with some stiffness and went back inside the trading post only to reappear moments later with a piece of parchment with two strings about eight inches long encrusted with sugar crystals and a cover for the pot.

---

[51] Literally "sweet rocks"
[52] Candy

Wôquhsak and Mushqeenupeeash stood as he approached and Wôquhsak accepted the sweet treat with one hand while handing the required three fathoms of wampum with the other and making a short bow to the agent. Mushqeenupeeash took the cover for the newly bartered pot from the agent's other hand. Wôquhsak placed the "sweet rocks" in his deerskin pouch, then looked toward where Jules had been standing to thank him for his help. Jules had moved away without requiring any thanks, but Wôquhsak now noticed something odd.

Wôquhsak had noticed a man standing at a distance from the trading post leaning against a tree watching intently as they made their trade. Unlike the figure leaning against the building and trying to seem uninterested in their trade, this wôpusu[53] was intently watching Jules as he participated in the trade.

It was this man that now approached Jules and engaged him in conversation. They were far enough away from Wôquhsak that he could not hear what was being said, but he could see that the man was persisting, and the words heated. Jules was attempting to walk away.

The man was not unknown to Wôquhsak. He was not considered a friend of the ununuwak[54]. This man was not just speaking to neetôpâwun[55] Jules, he was angry, berating Jules over something. Jules kept trying to walk away, but the man would not allow it. Jules raised his arms defensively and continued to back away from the man. The man persisted.

Wôquhsak was concerned by what he was seeing. He had heard it said this man, Devon by name, had once nearly beaten to death a confused elderly tribal member who had inadvertently wandered onto his property. His landholdings were near to those of Jules' who he now stood arguing with at the trading post. His name was Devon but known to most of the Narragansett people in the area as Devil Devon.

---

[53] White Man
[54] People – the Narragansett
[55] Friend

23

Wôquhsak saw Jules pull his cloak tighter about himself and turn his back to walk away from his aggressor. The man quickly stepped in front of Jules. Devon then pulled a folded piece of parchment from a pocket and thrust it against Jules' chest. Jules used his left arm to quickly push Devil's right arm aside, and saying something sharply inches from Devil's face, turned and walked away. The Devil was left standing there. He was seething with anger still holding his paper.

Mushqeenupeeash had gathered the bearskin and was waiting for Wôquhsak to indicate he was ready to pick up the newly purchased pot and go to the muhshoon[56]. A nudge from the edge of the bearskin under Mushqeenupeeash's arm brought Wôquhsak back out of his concern over what he had just witnessed.

As the two turned to leave, Wôquhsak could not stop himself from approaching the huddled figure beside the corner of the trading post.

"Neechay[57]," Wôquhsak said as he bent down to the form, "my brother, are you alright? Are you well? Why are you here?"

The figure recoiled from this show of concern by Wôquhsak, as if he expected to be struck. Wôquhsak was about to say something more when he heard the voice of Wilcox behind him.

"Leave him be," the voice boomed. "He's jest one of yer kind that's found himself in a bottle of whiskey."

Although Wôquhsak did not fully understand what Wilcox had said, it was said with such venom and disdain Wôquhsak knew not to pursue trying to talk to this wretch. As he rose to leave, Wôquhsak suddenly caught a glint in the eye of the cowering form that showed him all he had seen was an act.

Still wondering at what he had just seen and giving a final look back at the figure sitting on the ground, the two boys took hold of the pot handle and headed for their dugout.

---

[56] Dugout canoe
[57] Brother

With the muhshoon[58] emptied of the pelts, there was plenty of room for the cooking pot inside the woven reed basket. The two boys placed their prize in the center of the boat and covered it with the bearskin. They were both excited by the prospect of presenting the pot to Wôquhsak's mother. But first, there was the matter of a sweet treat to be consumed.

Settling in their places in the muhshoon[59], the boys used their wutahôqsak[60] to push off out of the marsh grass and begin to paddle back the way they had come.

---

[58] Dugout canoe
[59] Ibid footnote 58
[60] Paddles

THREE

THE MUHSHOON[61] CUT CLEANLY THROUGH THE CALM
waters of the cove. The paddles, powered by the strokes of the strong
young men, quickly increased the distance away from the trading post.
With every dip of the wutahôq[62], Wôquhsak relaxed a bit more. He had
been successful, but it had not been enjoyable. Traders were not
friends. The worst part was seeing one of their own disheveled and
besotted. The best part was seeing neetôpâwun[63] Jules.

"We beat them at their own game," Wôquhsak heard Mushqeenupeeash say with excitement.

"No, Mushqeenupeeash," Wôquhsak replied. "Traders always
win."

"But we have what we wanted," Mushqeenupeeash insisted, "and
we have wampum left with us. You even got shukanees[64] he did not
charge us for! You impress me, natôquhs. No other cousin of mine
could have traded so well."

---

61 Dugout canoe
62 Paddles
63 Literally, "our friend"
64 Rock candy

Wôquhsak stopped paddling and looked at Mushqeenupeeash's back as he paddled at the front of the muhshoon[65].

"Mushqeenupeeash," He said slightly confused, "you have no other natôquhsak[66]."

"Exactly," Mushqeenupeeash replied beginning to laugh. Wôquhsak laughed, as well. And so, the joke was acknowledged, and the mood was lightened.

They were now passing the trading post of friend Williams and were about to round the western end of the island in the cove. Wôquhsak started to look for a place to land along the shore of the cove and looked back toward the trading posts to be sure they were out of sight.

"Mushqeenupeeash," He quietly called out, "Head for the shore where that tall clump of marsh grass is. Just there along the shore."

Mushqeenupeeash pointed to where he thought Wôquhsak indicated and Wôquhsak nodded. Two or three more strokes and a drag from Wôquhsak's wutahôq[67] steering in the stern and the muhshoon[68] turned and slid into the shore amid the tallest clumps of marsh grass.

"Stay down," Wôquhsak cautioned.

"What are we doing," Mushqeenupeeash asked Wôquhsak?

"I am going to take you to a place my father showed me the last time we came to trade. But we need to hide our muhshoon[69] in the marsh grass while we are gone."

The two boys got out of the dugout, and, bending low, began putting dead marsh grass and a few branches that lay about over their boat. Wôquhsak pulled a loose clump of marsh grass out of the marshy shore and dropped it behind the stern of the boat to hide it from anyone passing on the water. Wôquhsak picked up his deerskin pouch with the shukanees[70] in it from inside the dugout and, warning

---

[65] Ibid Footnote 62
[66] Cousins
[67] Paddle
[68] Dugout canoe
[69] Ibid Footnote 68
[70] Candies

Mushqeenupeeash to stay low until they reached the tree line, began a crouched run to the trees.

Once at the tree line, Wôquhsak stopped to look back across the water to see if there were any indications they had been noticed. Not seeing any, he looked at Mushqeenupeeash and smiled.

"We will cross the trail a little further up the rise," he said to Mushqeenupeeash, "then up the hill on the other side. Stay close to me." Wôquhsak was enjoying feeling his position as leader.

The two young braves scurried through the trees and up the slight incline, reaching the edge of a clearing about fifteen feet wide. The center was well worn from many years of moccasin travel. There were two other less-worn tracks from wagon wheels of more recent origin. This was the Pequot Trail. Mushqeenupeeash had only seen it further south where it ran nearer the shore and was not sheltered by trees.

Wôquhsak stopped at the edge of the trail. Mushqeenupeeash followed his lead. The two of them looked for anything traveling on the trail. Nothing was in sight. Quickly, the two forms sprung from the underbrush and sprinted the short distance to the shelter of the brush on the far side of the trail. Picking his way up the steeper incline on this side of the trail, Wôquhsak led Mushqeenupeeash up to a ledge and, working his way to the end of it, climbed the fifteen or twenty feet to the flat top of the rock and into a break in the trees and glorious sunshine.

The two of them collapsed onto the warm exposed rock and drew deep breaths to ease their excitement and exhaustion. After a few moments, Wôquhsak sat up and opened his pouch. He unwrapped the parchment and handed Mushqeenupeeash his string of candy. The two of them lay back on the rock enjoying the warmth from the rock on their backs, sucking on their sweet candy, and listening to the birds and the rustling of the wind in the tree branches that would soon be in full leaf. A few of the trees were in early leaf, but nothing like the full leaf of summer.

As they lay in the sun, they talked quietly about how they would be greeted when they arrived back home. Wôquhsak's mother would shower them with hugs and tell all who were within hearing how her sons (for now Mushqeenupeeash was surely considered to be a son) had made the trip to the trading post alone and bought this beautiful iron pot. They giggled and tried to make their "sweet rocks" last as long as possible.

The birds were gleefully chirping when Wôquhsak suddenly heard a tweet that was not really a chirp from a bird. He hushed Mushqeenupeeash and cocked his head to hear the sound more clearly. It was not a bird that was making that sound. This was someone whistling. Wôquhsak rolled over and crawled to the edge of the flat rock that overlooked the Pequot Trail. Mushqeenupeeash did the same. He could hear the whistling getting closer and recognized the notes and the cadence. In a moment, he saw the figure of Jules dressed in his distinctive hat and cloak, walking south on the trail. He was headed home having left the trading post and whistling to himself as if he had not a care in the world.

As Jules reached the very center of their field of vision, another figure appeared behind Jules running to catch up to him. It was the same man who had argued heatedly with Jules at the trading post. The boys watched as Devon the Devil called to Jules, who stopped and turned to see who was behind him. They saw Jules once again being verbally attacked by the man. Soon, the paper they had seen before at the trading post appeared again in the hand of aggressor. Again, Jules pushed it away. Jules made a motion with his arms as if to say "enough!" and turned to continue his walk home.

The Devil stood without movement for a moment as Jules took a few steps moving away. Suddenly, the Devil reached behind him, and a Narragansett war club appeared in his hand, its two-foot curved wooden handle ending in a dark rounded stone ball. He ran toward Jules and, with one continuous move, pulled Jules' hat off with his left hand, and with his right, brought the pahqumuhq[71] down on the back of Jules' head. Jules dropped to his knees. His attacker brought the heavy club down again across the right side of his head and Jules fell to the ground.

Mushqeenupeeash was about to let out a cry that would have betrayed their presence when Wôquhsak grabbed him, covering his mouth, and rolling him back from the edge of the rock ledge. Wôquhsak whispered to Mushqeenupeeash to be silent. The two boys lay there for what seemed like minutes, afraid to make a sound. Wôquhsak was first to crawl carefully back to the edge of the ledge. What he saw, he did not understand. Devon was kneeling next to the fallen form of Jules and was lifting the dead man's hand to dip it in the blood pooling on the ground near Jules' head. Devon then pressed it against the paper that he now held in his hand. When he had finished doing this, he looked up and down the trail to be sure he was unseen.

When he was sure no one was in sight, he quickly stripped the red cloak from the lifeless form of Jules. Taking his victim by the boots, Devon pulled his victim to the edge of the trail and used the toe of his own boot to dismissively roll it into the bushes lining the east side of the trail. He watched as it fell down the incline and disappeared into the shrubs.

Once he assured himself the body was not visible from the trail, Devon gathered the maroon cloak, now with a darker stain of Jules' blood at the collar, and the hat of matching hue from where it had fallen on the trail. Wrapping the hat in the cloak, he came to the side of the trail where Wôquhsak and Mushqeenupeeash lay above him watching his every move.

It looked, for a moment, like Devon was going to climb up the ridge where the boys lay. Instead, he stopped at the base of the outcrop and stuffed the hat and cloak into a small hollow at the base of the outcrop. Again, he glanced up and down the trail to be sure he was

---

[71] A Narragansett war cub. Literally a 'head splitter'

30

alone, then sprinted down the trail leaving only the blooded war club on the side of the trail and his victim's blood soaking into the dirt of the trail.

Mushqeenupeeash joined his cousin to peer at the scene below them on the trail. They were frozen in place by what they had witnessed. Wôquhsak soon realized they needed to act. When Jules' body was discovered, the weapon would be identified as a Narragansett war club, and the immediate thought would be he was killed by an indigenous brave. The real killer would get away with his crime. It was then Wôquhsak knew he had to do something.

"Mushqeenupeeash," Wôquhsak said sternly, "I cannot explain all now, but do what I say now without question. We must be quick and quiet." Mushqeenupeeash, wide-eyed and obviously shaken, nodded his agreement. Wôquhsak swiftly descended from the rock, quickly picking his way down to the trail.

"Gather the cloak and hat," Wôquhsak instructed Mushqeenupeeash. "I will get the pahqumuhq[72]."

Mushqeenupeeash returned to the outcrop and pulled the cloak and hat carefully from their hiding place. He wrapped them carefully into a bundle and noticed the stain of blood near the collar. He carefully rolled it over his arm. The two of them stood near the edge of the trail on the side leading to the water.

"I think this is all we will need," Wôquhsak said breathlessly. "They will have a harder time determining who is responsible for this act."

"Will they?" Mushqeenupeeash questioned? "Look at the footprints we left with our mahusunash[73]!"

Mushqeenupeeash was right. The ground around the scene held the impressions of their moccasins, and where imprints of boots existed, they were overlayed with moccasin prints. Wôquhsak reached into the underbrush and picked up a short branch fallen in the winter from one of the trees and attempted to sweep away all the prints. He

---

[72] Narragansett war club. Literally 'head splitter'
[73] moccasins

could not obliterate all of them for there was a rising fear in him that someone might come down the trail at any moment and see the two of them. Taking a final sweep, Wôquhsak threw the branch into the underbrush and, lightly tapping Mushqeenupeeash's chest, bolted into the trees heading for the cove and their muhshoon[74].

The two young braves raced through the trees to the beginning of the marsh grass. They crouched low as they made their way through the tall grass along the edge of the cove until they reached their dugout. Wôquhsak and Mushqeenupeeash quickly threw aside the marsh grass and branches they had used earlier to hide the boat. With profound respect, they placed the cloak and hat inside the iron pot and re-covered it with the bearskin.

Giving a slight push on the bow of the dugout, it slid easily out of the marsh grass into the water. Wôquhsak backpaddled as Mushqeenupeeash settled in the bow. They guided the muhshoon[75] as far to the south side of the cove as possible hoping no one at the trading post on the north shore would notice them so far across the cove as they paddled for the open water. Wôquhsak kept watching in the direction of the trading post as they dug their paddles into the water in easy rhythm. He saw no sign of anyone looking back.

They rounded the point of the cove and entered the great bay. It was then that Wôquhsak realized Mushqeenupeeash was crying quietly in the bow of the craft.

"Why are you crying, Mushqeenupeeash?" Wôquhsak asked with concern.

"I am saddened that we have lost a good friend of our people," Mushqeenupeeash replied. "We must tell the foreigners what one of them did," he said quietly through his tears.

The current in the bay was now running with them as water left the bay and Wôquhsak rested on his paddle and considered how to reply to his cousin.

---

[74] Dugout canoe
[75] Ibid Footnote 74

"Mushqeenupeeash," He said after a few moments, "what would they do if we accused one of their own of this murder? You know they would not believe us. We are the savages, and this is a savage act. And the weapon is one of our making."

"But he needs to be punished," Mushqeenupeeash replied, his tears now being replaced by anger. "This man has committed an evil act and must answer for it!"

"I understand your anger, natôquhs[76]. I am angry too," Wôquhsak said calmly. "But we must realize we cannot accuse him directly without admitting that we were there and saw the act. Then it could become a question of our words against his and who would be believed? No, we must find another way."

"Then why did you have us take the hat and cloak and the bloody pahqumuhq[77]?" Mushqeenupeeash questioned. "Does our having them not make us look guilty of the crime?"

"Do you not understand, Mushqeenupeeash," Wôquhsak replied. "We cannot tell anyone we saw what happened. The only way this man will receive justice is this: he must confess the act himself."

"No man will do that, especially one with as dark a soul as he has," Mushqeenupeeash said, scoffing at the thought.

"Then we will need to find a way to make him want to confess," Wôquhsak said quietly.

Mushqeenupeeash caught Wôquhsak's eyes and saw something he had never seen before. It was a steeliness of purpose, a mulling over of the situation, and the germ of a plan evolving before his eyes.

"Wôquhsak," Mushqeenupeeash said, "you are giving me concern. What is it that you are planning?"

"I am not quite sure yet," Wôquhsak replied without changing his expression. "But you are right, natôquhs[78], I am working on a plan."

---

[76] Cousin
[77] Narragansett war club. Literally 'head splitter'
[78] Cousin

As the two young men drifted along with the current, their excitement over the gift for Wôquhsak 's mother had been overshadowed by other events of the day. As they began to paddle again, it was not with the purposeful strokes of the morning, but with a more relaxed rhythm. Neither wanted to speak, and so they paddled in silence, the cloak and hat out of sight in the pot covered by the lid and bearskin sitting securely in the middle of their dugout.

The wind had died completely and the water near the shore was like glass reflecting the shoreline and sky with the quality of a mirror. The sun was still high enough in the sky that the shadow cast from the rising bank to the west was still small against the shore. Wôquhsak and Mushqeenupeeash were quietly paddling. Every dip into the water drew an eddy of water as the paddle was pulled back against the dugout. All was quiet, until Wôquhsak began to softly whistle a melody. It was neetôpâwun[79] Jules' song, the one he always whistled. Mushqeenupeeash began to whistle, as well. He was not as practiced as Wôquhsak, but he wanted to improve. He missed a note here and there, but he was determined to get the melody down.

And so, they paddled on toward the summer camp of their clan softly whistling the notes and coordinating the strokes of their paddles with the cadence of the song.

---

[79] Friend

FOUR

THEY ARRIVED AT THE SUMMER VILLAGE WHILE THE SUN was still well above the hills to the west. Wôquhsak and Mushqeenupeeash pulled the muhshoon[80] up on the sandy beach and realized their exhaustion. Any remnant of excitement for the successful completion of their trip was not evident either on their faces or their demeanor.

"We must not show how we are feeling to our mother," Wôquhsak said as they emptied the muhshoon[81]. "We have to show our mother happy and excited faces."

"I do not feel that now," Mushqeenupeeash replied.

"Whether you do or not, you must show it," Wôquhsak insisted. "Do not worry, natôquhs[82], I know how we will get justice for neetôpâwun[83] Jules. Trust me and play along."

They placed their paddles in the dugout and lifted the bearskin and the woven basket beneath it out of the boat.

"We must hide the cloak and hat where they will not be discovered," Wôquhsak whispered to Mushqeenupeeash, "and the war club. Let us put it all under the bearskin where the pelts were at the side of

---

[80] Dugout canoe
[81] Ibid Footnote 80
[82] Cousin
[83] Our friend

35

the shelter, if only temporarily." Mushqeenupeeash nodded in agreement.

Reaching under the bearskin, the two boys reached for the handle of the basket. Wôquhsak picked up the blood-spattered pahqumuhq[84] in his left hand and, holding it close to his leg and the pot between them, they walked slowly toward their lodge. The iron pot seemed heavier than when they had carried it to their dugout at the trading post. The cloak and hat could not have added that much more weight to be carried. Was it the strain of paddling they were feeling in their arm muscles? Or was it only a betrayal of their somber mood?

They reached their lodge and quickly went around the corner to the more secluded side. The place where the basket had been that morning was still empty. They placed the basket back where it had been earlier. Wôquhsak quickly threw the bearskin aside and removed the cover from the pot. Taking the new iron pot out of the basket, he placed Jules' cloak and hat inside the basket, along with the war club, The cover for the basket lay beside it on the ground and Wôquhsak quickly placed it on the basket. Mushqeenupeeash and Wôquhsak stood for a moment to recover their strength.

"We must show only happiness and immense joy at presenting our honored mother with our gift," Wôquhsak said trying to catch his breath. The two of them looked at each other and nodded: they were ready. Mushqeenupeeash picked up the bearskin and the two again hoisted the heavy pot with its cover and brought it around to the front of the lodge, setting it about five feet in front of the door. Mushqeenupeeash covered it with the bearskin.

"Quhtchânumuwee noohkâs[85], we have something for you," Wôquhsak spoke in a loud commanding voice, gaining the attention of all nearby. "Please come out to see."

Wôquhsak's mother appeared in the doorway. She had never heard her son speak in such a manner. Tentatively, she came out into the

---

[84] Narragansett war club. Literally 'head splitter'
[85] Honored Mother

fading daylight. Wôquhsak poked Mushqeenupeeash and gave his mother his biggest smile. Mushqeenupeeash managed to do the same.

"Honored Mother," he repeated, "we have made a trip to the trading post of the wôpusuwak[86] this day and return to give you a gift we know you desire and need." Wôquhsak made a gesture to Mushqeenupeeash to pull back the bearskin. Wôquhsak's mother brought her hands to her mouth and gasped as her eyes focused on the new iron pot.

"My sons," she gasped. "Such a gift! You give me immense joy!"

The woman approached her young men and clasped them in a hug. She was so small against them. Everyone had gathered around them and was admiring the new iron cooking pot. Wôquhsak hugged his mother and saw the smile on Mushqeenupeeash's face beginning to fade. He could not hide his feelings as well as Wôquhsak.

"Let us carry the pot inside for you," Wôquhsak said to his mother, looking at Mushqeenupeeash for his help. "Then Mushqeenupeeash and I must speak with the Elders about something," he said looking at Mushqeenupeeash.

The two boys lifted the iron pot and carried it inside the lodge, its weight no longer an issue. Once inside, Wôquhsak's mother guided them to a spot near the far wall and motioned for them to set the pot there. She was already preparing the evening meal and told the boys to be seated.

She had grilled some fish caught by members of the clan that day. The fillets were boned expertly and grilled to a fine brown shade. Wôquhsak's mother had grilled the fillets with some wild herbs that added great flavor. She had also prepared a corn mash. As tasty and filling as the food was, it did little to lighten the mood of the two young braves.

---

[86] White Men

When Wôquhsak's mother left the fire circle. Mushqeenupeeash turned to his cousin and angrily whispered, "Why did you say we were going to see the Elders? What are they going to do for us?"

"Perhaps nothing," Wôquhsak whispered in return, "but I want to see how they will react to my plan if I can disguise it in my explanation."

"You haven't even told me what this plan is!" Mushqeenupeeash grumbled under his breath.

"Don't worry, I will," Wôquhsak whispered just as his mother returned to the fire ring with more food. He looked at her and returned her warm smile with his own. Mushqeenupeeash took another taste of the fish.

Once the meal was ended, Wôquhsak was asked by his mother, "Why are you seeking the advice of the Elders?" It was a question he was not sure how to answer.

"Noohkâs[87], today on our trip," Wôquhsak began, "Mushqeenupeeash and I saw something that disturbed us." He tried to choose his words carefully. "We all know the wôpusuwak[88] can be violent toward us. Yet today we saw one injure another badly. He did so in a way that would lead other white men to lay blame upon one of us." Wôquhsak did not want to upset his mother by saying they had seen a murder. Mushqeenupeeash sat quietly, hanging on every word.

"I want to ask the Kuhchâyak[89] if there is something we should do since Mushqeenupeeash and I were the only ones to witness this act. We want the great Manutoo[90] to look favorably upon us," Wôquhsak concluded.

His mother sat quietly listening and said nothing for a few moments. She then turned to her son and said, "You are right to bring this to the Elders. They should know what has occurred, especially if

---

[87] Mother
[88] White Men
[89] Elders
[90] Great Spirit

it could be thought the act was done by one of our tribe members. Go and seek their advice with my blessing."

Wôquhsak thanked his mother for her sage advice and motioned to Mushqeenupeeash to get ready to leave. They slipped through the door, again thanking Wôquhsak's mother, and walked across the middle area of the camp to the lodge of the clan Elders. As they walked, Mushqeenupeeash told Wôquhsak how impressed he was with his explanation to his mother.

"I did not lie," Wôquhsak said. "I only colored the truth to spare her the worst part. I will not do that before the Kuhchâyak[91]. They must know the whole truth."

The boys reached the door of the Elders' meeting lodge and Wôquhsak paused to take a deep breath. He called out to the Elders within for permission to enter. A voice from inside bid the two boys to enter.

Within the lodge, a fire circle cast strange, oversized shadows against the birch bark walls. The five Elders sat around the fire with great solemnity. These men were known to Mushqeenupeeash and Wôquhsak, but the presence of these young braves before these weathered wisemen of the clan, under these circumstances, required the discussion be of a serious nature. Even if there were familial relations with any of these men, it was not important in this setting. Here, the Elders spoke for the good of the entire clan.

"Kuhchâyak[92]," Wôquhsak began as he sat cross legged on the side of the fire nearest the entrance to the lodge, "Mushqeenupeeash and I come to you for your wise advice."

"Continue," said the oldest of the Elders.

Wôquhsak began explaining about their trip to the trading post and buying the iron pot for his mother. He told them about seeing neetôpâwun[93] Jules, who they knew well, and the help he had rendered

---

[91] Elders
[92] Ibid Footnote 91
[93] Friend

them. He told them about stopping on the big rock outcrop after leaving the trading post and enjoying their skukanees[94] sweets.

"This is all interesting and we are sure was exciting for you," the elder spoke in a kindly tone, "but why does this bring you here to speak with us?"

"It is what happened while we were on the big rock," Wôquhsak began again. "Neetôpâwun[95] Jules came walking down the great trail whistling and was approached by the same man we had seen start an argument with Jules at the trading post. He had a piece of paper he kept pushing at our friend and, I think, he wanted his mark on it. Neetôpâwun[96] Jules pushed it away and began walking again."

"This is none of our affair," another of the Elders offered, disgruntled.

"It is what happened next, wise Kuhchâyak[97] that we come to you about," Wôquhsak replied. "When neetôpâwun Jules turned from his pursuer and began walking, his pursuer attacked him with a pahqumuhq[98]! He is dead."

The Elders groaned and collectively shook their heads.

"Are you sure of this?" one of the Elders said anxiously. "Neetôpâwun Jules is dead?"

"It is so," Wôquhsak assured them. "He was struck with one of our war clubs."

"One curious thing did occur," Wôquhsak added. "Before the killer ran from the scene, he dipped one of Jules' fingers in the blood pooling on the ground and touched it to the paper he had been pushing at our friend Jules."

"This is none of our affair." the first Elder spoke again. "What is it you seek from us?"

---

[94] Candy
[95] Friend
[96] Ibid Footnote 95
[97] Elders
[98] Narragansett war club. Literally 'head splitter'

"I fear we will be blamed for this act," Wôquhsak replied, "because of the weapon used and footprints at the scene. We had to cross near the body to get back to the cove and our boat."

"You left your moccasin prints near the body?" another Elder questioned.

"We tried to wipe them out with a branch, but may have missed some," Mushqeenupeeash blurted out.

"May I continue," Wôquhsak spoke up as the Elders began muttering about the situation among themselves. "We all know, if we go to the wôpusuwak[99], they will not believe us. Instead, they will blame us rather than believe one of their own would do such a thing as kill one of their own, especially using a Narragansett weapon. Mushqeenupeeash and I have a plan."

The announcement of a plan by these two boys drew the interest of the Elders.

"You all know the only way for the wôpusuwak[100] to accept that one of their own committed this murder is to hear it from the murderer himself. He must confess his deed," Wôquhsak said forcefully. This statement caused a great clamor of discussion among the Elders.

"But, how do you propose to have him do so?" the lead Elder asked.

"Neetôpâwun[101] Jules always wore his red cape and his hat that any who knew him would recognize," Wôquhsak began his answer. All the Elders nodded in agreement.

"Mushqeenupeeash and I have taken Jules' cloak and hat," Wôquhsak stated somberly. "We also have the pahqumuhq[102] with our friend's blood on it."

"Why would you take these things from the scene of the killing?" the Elders questioned.

---

[99] White Men
[100] White Men
[101] Friend
[102] Narragansett war club. Literally 'head splitter'

"It is part of my plan," Wôquhsak replied confidently. "We all agree the killer must confess his crime for him to be believed. We will get him to confess."

"I, for one, do not understand how you will do this," said the most senior of the Elders.

"We will convince him Keetanut[103] is haunting him for his evil deed," Wôquhsak responded. "He will see what he thinks is the ghost of Jules, he will hear sounds and see the weapon he used everywhere he looks. He will hear the one thing Jules alone always did, and he will hear it everywhere. It will be the tune Jules always whistled. We will drive him to confess from his own fear."

"What do you wish from us, young brave?" the same Elder asked.

"I ask you to help us in any way we may ask because we do this to keep our people safe from the revenge the wôpusuwak[104] may seek, believing we committed this killing."

---

[103] The Creator
[104] White Men

FIVE

WÔQUHSAK AND MUSHQEENUPEEASH STOOD OUTSIDE the lodge of the Elders in the cool early summer evening air and felt very grown up. They had met with the Elders and presented their plan to protect the tribe. They had won the approval of the Elders to implement their plan to deceive the killer, Devon, into believing he was being haunted by his victim.

"You still have not told me what the plan actually is, Wôquhsak," Mushqeenupeeash put the question to Wôquhsak as they walked back to their lodge.

"I am still working on some of it," Wôquhsak replied. "The first step, I think, is to learn as much about Devon as possible so we can use it to our advantage against him."

"What do we do if the wôpusuwak[105] are swift to want revenge and blame us?" Mushqeenupeeash questioned. "They will surely find the body soon. Many travel the trail."

"That is why we must quickly learn all we can about Devon's nature, his daily life," Wôquhsak replied. "We must learn if anyone knows him well enough to give us this knowledge of him."

---

[105] White Men

43

Wôquhsak's mother was waiting for them when they returned from meeting with the Elders. She was anxious to know what was said, Wôquhsak did not want to tell her any more than was necessary to calm any fears she had. He did tell her the Elders had agreed to help if asked. He asked her if she knew of anyone who might know the wôpusuwak[106] called Devon. She thought this was an odd question but responded by telling her son that she knew of a woman from another clan, whose summer camp was not far, who was rumored to have worked for the wôpusu[107] Devon.

"Do you want to speak with her?" Wôquhsak's mother questioned.

"No," replied Wôquhsak feigning little interest. "It was a question I was asked by the Elders."

Hearing this, Mushqeenupeeash winced at the lie Wôquhsak had just spoken. Wôquhsak snapped a look of "say nothing" in Mushqeenupeeash's direction and suggested it was late and time for sleep. As they laid down among the covers of animal skins, Wôquhsak whispered to Mushqeenupeeash that, even if he did not fully understand the plan, he must not show that reaction should he hear something unknown to him. Mushqeenupeeash was angered slightly by his cousin's words, but he knew Nupanawôquhsak[108] would eventually tell him everything once he had worked all the details out.

Morning brought an end to the tossing and restless sleep Wôquhsak experienced. The thought of how to make Devon admit to his crime kept Wôquhsak's mind working on the plan over and over while he tried to sleep. Many of the uncertainties needed to become known for the plan to come together.

Wôquhsak rose and went to wash his face and body as he did every morning. He returned to the lodge to find Mushqeenupeeash just opening his eyes to the morning light. Wôquhsak's mother was just stirring the embers of the fire.

---

[106] White Men
[107] White Man
[108] Five Red Foxes

"Dress, cousin," Wôquhsak said to Mushqeenupeeash quietly. "We must see this woman who can tell us something of our killer."

It took Mushqeenupeeash only moments to wash and dress. The two of them gobbled down a few cakes of cornmeal freshly grilled over the morning fire by Wôquhsak's mother. As they ate the warm cakes, Wôquhsak casually talked to his mother about the woman she had mentioned the night before who might have worked for this wôpusu[109] Devon.

"Her name I believe is Sôqanupee (Cool Water)," Upeeshâ-wônkoon said to her son. "Her clan's summer camp is not far. Why are you asking me this?"

"No reason," Wôquhsak said feigning he had no interest really. "Devon was mentioned by the Elders, and I did not know much about him." Mushqeenupeeash winced as he heard another half-truth pass his cousin's lips.

Quickly changing the subject, Wôquhsak told his mother the two of them were going to go fishing for dinner. His mother reminded him that his father was likely to be returning in a day or two and not to bring home too many fish. Once more, Mushqeenupeeash knew Wôquhsak had lied to his mother. Her good-natured chiding was in jest, of course, and both boys smiled at her in response. As they left the lodge, they each took a fishing line and put them in the leather pouches they carried slung over their shoulders and across their chests.

The summer camp of Sôqanupee lay more than a mile, but less than two, from the summer camp of Wôquhsak's clan. Having told his mother they were going fishing, Wôquhsak and Mushqeenupeeash headed for the shore. They launched the same muhshoon[110] they had used the day before and turned south along the shoreline. It would only take one movement of the sun to paddle the muhshoon[111] around

---

[109] White Man
[110] Dugout canoe
[111] Ibid Footnote 110

45

the slight point of land that protected the summer camp of Wôquh-sak's clan and come within sight of the summer camp of Sôqanupee's people.

As the young braves approached the camp, they raised their paddles over their heads in a show of coming in peace. They were greeted as the dugout slid into the sand of the shore by one of the tribal Elders.

"Tah wuchee puyômân[112]?" was their greeting from the Elder.

"I have come to speak with one of your mutumuhsuhs," Wôquh-sak replied, "Sôqanupee. Is she here?"

"What do you want of her?" the Elder asked.

"I need to ask her about someone she may know," Wôquhsak replied calmly. "She may know how I can reach this person."

Mushqeenupeeash listened carefully to the words Wôquhsak spoke. He recognized the truth behind the words spoken and knew the Elder, for all his wisdom, would not understand the true meaning.

"Sôqanupee should be at work in the garden," the Elder offered. "You are welcome to speak with her, but do not keep her from her work."

"Wunâyush, Kuhchâyuhs,"[113] Wôquhsak thanked the Elder, wishing him to "be well."

Wôquhsak and Mushqeenupeeash walked casually through the camp toward the extensive garden they could see on the far side of the camp, smiling at those who occasionally noticed them as strangers. Several mutumuhsuhs[114] were diligently working cultivating the rows of early corn and beans. The two boys had no idea which of these women was the one they sought. Standing at the edge of the planted rows, Wôquhsak called out, "Sôqanupee? Are you here?"

A woman about midway down a row, stood from her crouched position and looked in the direction of the voice calling her name.

---

[112] "What come you for"
[113] "Be Well, Elder" (man)
[114] Woman. The term "squaw" is a loan word adapted into American English from Algonquin

46

"I am here," came the reply. "Who calls me?"

Wôquhsak and Mushqeenupeeash sprinted down the side of the garden to where Sôqanupee was walking to meet them wiping the dark earth from her hands. Wôquhsak introduced himself and Mushqeenupeeash and asked if he might ask her a question or two about a wôpusu[115] she might have worked for at one time. She nodded in agreement.

Before he began with his first question, he cautioned the woman that their conversation must remain secret, and, though others will be curious about what they spoke about, she must not reveal the nature of the subject of their discussion. Cautiously, the woman agreed, feeling a bit afraid. Wôquhsak tried to calm the look of fear that was showing in her eyes.

"Please, Sôqanupee, understand the information we seek is important to all our people," Wôquhsak said with a plea in his voice.

Sôqanupee was not young. Her complexion showed many years of long days in the sun. She was widowed many years now and she had no children. The rest of her clan cared for her needs but did not care about her. She had a bitterness about her that reflected how she felt.

"Do you know a wôpusu[116] called Devon?" Wôquhsak asked.

"Devon?" Sôqanupee questioned in reply. "I know him. He is machusuw[117] in the head. Why do you ask about such a bad person?"

"Did you once work for him?" Wôquhsak ignored her question.

"I worked in his filthy house last winter when we needed food," she replied spitting in disgust. "He has a sickness in the brain, kakeewâw[118]. He desires much, envies what others possess, but does not want to work for the same. You would be best served to leave him alone!"

"Is he a believer in manutoowak[119]?" Wôquhsak asked.

---

[115] White Man
[116] White Man
[117] "Bad in the head"
[118] "crazy in the head"
[119] spirits

47

"Devon?" Sôqanupee replied. "He fears anything he cannot see or easily explain. His mind fears the dark. He is violent."

"Where does he live?" Wôquhsak asked casually.

"He has a small cabin over the rise beyond the trail," Sôqanupee responded pointing in the direction of the trail. "You cannot miss it. It is not cared for and looks abandoned. But he is looking to move to another place. That is what he told me when he no longer wanted me to work this spring. He is a neighbor of neetôpâwun[120] Jules, you know."

"Why do you tell me this?" Wôquhsak questioned.

"Devon is very jealous of Jules," the squaw replied. "Devon says Jules has better land than he has, and people respect Jules because he is not like the others. You know he speaks with a different voice than the others and Devon envies the way he is accepted."

"Thank you for your words, Sôqanupee," Wôquhsak replied. "Please do not share what we have spoken about with anyone else," Wôquhsak cautioned. "If you are asked, as I can see others around us are curious to know why we speak, you can tell them we were asking if you could come to our camp to share one of your recipes with our mother, Upeeshâwônkoon (Snow Flower). You know her, do you not?"

"Yes," Sôqanupee replied with a small smile. "I remember her kindness when I was widowed. You are her sons? She is very lucky to have you. I will keep our words secret."

Bowing in respect, Wôquhsak and Mushqeenupeeash turned to leave. As they left the garden, Wôquhsak leaned toward Mushqeenupeeash and said, "I think I know how to make my plan work."

As they reached the beach and prepared to push their boat into the water, Mushqeenupeeash turned to Wôquhsak and said," Please tell me however much of the plan you have already conceived as you can. I am blind."

---

[120] Friend

"Let us get out from shore and I will tell you how we will accomplish our task," Wôquhsak said.

A dozen strong strokes with their paddles swiftly moved their dugout far enough from the shore that Wôquhsak was sure his voice would not carry to the shore. He rested his wutahoq[121] across the sides of the muhshoon[122] and told Mushqeenupeeash to stop paddling.

"You asked me what my plan is," Wôquhsak said quietly to him. "It is to make the murderer Devon confess his deed by making him believe the Great Manutoo[123] has been angered and turned against him. That He, the Great Spirit, is not allowing the soul of Jules to rest until Devon confesses his guilt."

Mushqeenupeeash thought a moment before saying, "you want him to believe the soul of neetôpâwun[124] Jules will not rest until he tells the truth?"

"Sôqanupee told us Devon has a suspicious mind and will be frightened by what he cannot explain. She also told us he planned to move. I wonder if that would be to Jules' cabin?" Wôquhsak said thinking aloud. "We must see if this has happened and scout the land surrounding the cabin."

"But Wôquhsak," Mushqeenupeeash questioned, "you still have not told me what the plan is. How will we make Devon want to confess?"

"We will do things to play with his mind, make him think he hears and sees things that are not, until he is driven by his guilt to tell the other wôpusuwak[125] what he did," Wôquhsak replied. "Then the wôpusuwak[126] with swords will come and take Devon away."

Mushqeenupeeash was satisfied by these words and, together, they began paddling again heading for home. The day was still young, and

---

[121] Paddle
[122] Dugout canoe
[123] Great Spirit
[124] Friend
[125] White Men
[126] Ibid Footnote 125

they needed to fish along the way. Wôquhsak's mother knew her son and his companion were too good at fishing not to bring home a catch. They dropped their fishing lines into the water and let them drift behind their boat as they paddled slowly along.

SIX

WÔQUHSAK AND MUSHQEENUPEEASH GENTLY GUIDED
the muhshoon[127] onto the beach at their clan's summer encampment
as the afternoon sun was still high in the sky. They were pleased with
the success of their trip. Sôqanupee had given them useful information
regarding Devon, information they would be able to use against him.
The string of tatawâqak[128] Mushqeenupeeash lifted out of the boat
were fat. These tautog[129] would make a satisfying meal for many of the
tribe.

They walked confidently through the camp with their catch in view
of everyone they passed. They reached their bark covered lodge expecting to find their mother pleased at their return and happy about
the bounty of their catch. Instead, they found Upeeshâwônkoon wor-
ried and upset.

"Mother," Wôquhsak said dropping his bag and rushing to her,
"what is wrong?"

"A message came for you from the Elders while you were away,"
Upeeshâwônkoon stammered in a shaky voice. "What did you speak
to the elders about, Wôquhsak?"

---

[127] Dugout canoe
[128] Several of a type of fish
[129] Ibid Footnote 128

"What was the message, mother?" Wôquhsak asked.

"The Elders want to see you as soon as you return, my son. What is going on?"

"Let me go speak with the Elders before I say anything, mother," Wôquhsak replied, trying to hold back any concern in his voice."

"I want to know what is said when you return," Upeeshâwônkoon had concern in her voice. Wôquhsak nodded and ducked through the doorway with Mushqeenupeeash trailing right behind.

The two young braves walked quickly, but not too quickly, through the camp to the lodge of the Elders. As they walked through the camp, Wôquhsak caught sight of someone slinking along the edge of the camp that was attempting to avoid them. Wôquhsak only saw the face for a few seconds, but he thought he recognized the individual as the figure that had been at the trading post the day they had gone to trade crouched against the building. The figure was out of sight behind one of the lodges before Wôquhsak could be sure.

They paused at the door and requested permission to enter from the guard at the door. Wôquhsak thought it odd that the Elders now had a guard. Wôquhsak turned to Mushqeenupeeash in the few moments they had before entering.

"I do not know what has happened but show no reaction to anything that is said," he said to Mushqeenupeeash who nodded his understanding.

In response to their request to enter, a voice from within the neesquta[130] summoned Wôquhsak and Mushqeenupeeash. The young braves were bidden to sit before the fire opposite the Elders. The leader of the Elders spoke first.

"Word has come to us that neetôpâwun[131] Jules body has not been found," he said with gravity. "When it is discovered, it will be as you told us. A runner will come to say the wôpusuwak[132] have begun

---

[130] Two fire longhouse
[131] Friend
[132] White Men

searching villages for the two young braves who were at the trading post the last time Jules was seen. The white men do not know which village these braves were from, so they will be searching every village."

"They will be here soon," Wôquhsak spoke up. The Elder continued.

"You did not blot out your moccasin prints as well as you might have. They will know Jules was hit on the head with something like a war club. They will not understand why his cloak and hat were taken. You have these along with the pahqumuhq[133], do you not?" Wôquhsak nodded his agreement.

"You must leave the camp," the second Elder said, "and take these things with you. Should the wôpusuwak[134] find these things here, they will not hesitate to kill everyone with their swords and fire sticks. You are a danger to any village, so do not seek shelter from any. The two of you must find a place to hide."

"When you came to us before, you asked us to help you," the first Elder spoke calmly, "You said you had a plan to make the killer come forward. What help do you seek?"

"For now, wise Kuhchâyak[135], I ask only two things," Wôquhsak answered in a strong yet unemotional voice. "I understand we have put the people of this village, and all villages, at great risk, so we will leave today. I ask our best weapon maker to see the pahqumuhq[136] that killed neetôpâwun[137] Jules and make us two like it."

The Elders turned to each other, and after a brief discussion, the oldest Elder turned to Wôquhsak and nodded his agreement.

"You asked for two things," he said softly. "What is the second?"

"Protect my mother," Wôquhsak replied. "Once my father returns, I will contact him, but he must not search for me. It would be too

---

[133] Narragansett war club. Literally 'head splitter'
[134] White Men
[135] Elder
[136] Narragansett war club. Literally, 'head splitter'
[137] Friend

dangerous for anyone to know where we are hiding. For now, every member of the village must forget us. It is to protect them."

"Should the wôpusuwak[138] come searching for two young braves," the Elder replied, "they will be told no such youths belong to this camp. Now you must leave before the sun sets."

Wôquhsak and Mushqeenupeeash stood and gave a small bow to the counsel.

"Wunâyuq[139]," the second Elder said to the two braves. Wôquhsak turned to face the Elder who spoke and wished him to be well also.

"Where will we go?" Mushqeenupeeash asked as they walked back through the camp to their lodge. "We are a danger to all the people now. I am beginning to think we made a mistake getting involved."

Wôquhsak stopped and turned to face Mushqeenupeeash.

"We would have been involved anyway," he said sternly. "Do you not see that all the people are in danger just because the wôpusuwak[140] are being fooled. Ahqee asookush[141], as well! We need to begin my plan as soon as possible. So, we must leave quickly to protect our village."

They reached their lodge and found Wôquhsak's mother standing at the doorway waiting for them. Wôquhsak embraced her and hurried her inside holding her hand. She looked at his face with fear in her eyes.

"Mother, Mushqeenupeeash and I must leave to protect everyone here," Wôquhsak began. "When we went to the trading post and bought your new pot, we saw our good friend Jules killed by another. It was not done by the hand of one of our people, but by a wôpusu[142]; one known to us. He used one of our weapons."

Upeeshâwônkoon gave out a small gasp and brought her hands to her face in horror.

---

[138] White Men
[139] "Be well"
[140] White Men
[141] Don't be foolish!
[142] White Man

"Mushqeenupeeash and I took the hat and cloak of our friend Jules, along with the pahqumuhq[143] used to strike and kill him," Wôquhsak continued. "We have them here, outside, hidden. The Elders have been told the wôpusuwak[144] have not yet found the body of our friend Jules but will be searching for the two young braves who were seen at the trading post when it is found. They do not know Jules was attacked and killed yet. That is why we must leave quickly."

"No, my son," Upeeshâwakoon wailed quietly. "You did nothing to have to run!"

"Mother," Wôquhsak replied softly, "should the white men come here and find us and Jules' belonging, they would kill the entire village. We must leave to protect everyone."

"Do not fear," Mushqeenupeeash spoke up. "I will see Wôquhsak is safe. And besides, he has a plan to make the killer confess."

This gave Upeeshâwônkoon a moment of pause. She then pulled her two young men into a strong embrace. She kissed each on the forehead and ushered them out the doorway. Wôquhsak turned back to his mother and said, "Mother, you must hide the new pot until it is safe again. If the wôpusuwak[145] see it, they will know those they seek came from this village."

The late afternoon sun was warm, but neither of the young braves had time to appreciate the warming rays. They turned at the corner of the lodge and uncovered the basket containing the hat and cloak of their friend Jules and the war club wrapped within it. They decided it would be easier to take the basket and would keep its content away from watchful eyes. Picking the basket up by its handles, the two braves turned back to the front of the lodge where Wôquhsak's mother was waiting before the doorway.

She handed each of them their carry bags that she had filled with some of their clothes and a day or two of food. They each thanked her

---

[143] Narragansett war club. Literally, 'head splitter'
[144] Ibid Footnote 139
[145] White Men

and, giving her a last embrace, headed for the edge of the camp clearing.

Just as they were entering the woods, they saw an older brave approaching them whom they recognized. His name was Kôkôch (Crow), and he walked with a noticeable limp from an injury he had sustained many years before. But his importance to the clan could not be doubted for he was the maker of weapons. In his right hand he carried a bow, and a quiver of arrows was slung on his back.

"Kuweeqahsun[146], Wôquhsak," He said as he approached, "I hope it is a good day for you. I come from the Elders to see what it is you need. They asked that I bring you these as you might need them," he continued.

Wôquhsak, at first, was slightly taken aback by the openness of Kôkôch's words. But knowing he had been sent by the Elders reassured him enough to share with him what he wanted. Reaching into the basket Wôquhsak and Mushqeenupeeash had set on the ground, Wôquhsak brought out the pahqumuhq[147] and held it before him using two hands to cradle it.

Kôkôch began examining the war club carefully.

"May I touch it?" he asked.

"Yes, of course," Wôquhsak replied.

"I see it is not of my making," Kôkôch said thoughtfully. "Although it is well made, the weight is not balanced. I see it has been used and was not cleaned after." He continued to examine the club, turning it over as he held it and swinging it in a downward motion several times.

"What is it you wish me to do?" he said looking at Wôquhsak finally.

"I want to know if you can make two the same as this," Wôquhsak replied. "I want them to look as close to this one as possible, even though this is not up to the quality of your work."

---

[146] "You continue to be in the light" – a form of good day
[147] Narragansett war club Literally, 'head splitter'

"But I could make it so much better," Kôkôch began, but Wôquh-sak cut him off.

"I know you can make it much better. But, no, they must be as close to this one as you can make them. How long will you need to make two like this one?"

Kôkôch thought for a moment as he rubbed his chin with one hand while he held the pahqumuhq[148] in the other.

"The Elders' council told me to do whatever you asked as quickly as possible, to put all other projects aside," Crow said deep in thought. "I have some pieces I can use.... I will need to form some pieces.... Give me three moon rises, and I will have them ready if you can give me this one to work from."

Wôquhsak was concerned about leaving the war club at camp. If the wôpusuwak[149] came and found it in their search, they would ask no question as they wiped out the camp.

"If I leave it with you, you must promise to keep it hidden," Wôquhsak cautioned Crow. "Should the wôpusuwak[150] come, they must not find it. Swear to the Great Manutoo[151] you will be cautious."

"How will I get these to you when they are done?" Crow asked.

"We will come to you," Wôquhsak replied.

Crow nodded his understanding and turned to leave, taking the war club, and sliding it inside his legging and covering it with his tunic. Wôquhsak and Mushqeenupeeash watched for a moment as Crow walked away. They looked about the camp, then at each other. Each of them took hold of the basket's handles and, with the quiver on Mushqeenupeeash back and the bow in hand, the two braves walked out of the camp clearing and into the woods.

---

[148] Narragansett war club. Literally, 'head splitter'
[149] White Men
[150] Ibid Footnote 148
[151] Spirit

SEVEN

DEVON SLOWED HIS PACE AFTER A FEW MINUTES OF trotting. He had passed a point in the trail where the path took a slight bend. He began to feel the adrenaline drain from his body as his breathing slowed. As his gait slowed to a walk, he swung his arms. He noticed a few spots of blood on the back of his right hand. He wondered if he was careless when he dipped the finger of his victim into the pooled blood on the ground. Suddenly he thought about the piece of paper and reached into his pocket to be sure it was there. Feeling the folded paper, he relaxed even more. He would finally now have what he had coveted for so long.

His mind wandered to the plan he had so carefully crafted that could now be realized. For several months he had begun spreading the story among his associates that Jules was going to leave for home and was going to sell his holdings to Devon. The well-respected, well-accepted Jules de Vendome had had enough of life in America's colonies and was returning home and would enrich his neighbor by selling everything he held to Devon. And the paper in his pocket was the proof that the sale had been concluded, signed, and sealed with Jules' mark and his fingerprint in blood. But the additional bonus was never having to hear that tune incessantly being whistled everywhere Jules went. He would say it reminded him of his home in Vendome where the carillon in the church played the melody every day.

These thoughts were flowing rapidly through his mind when he suddenly realized he was approaching the fine structure he would soon be moving into with its productive fields. He stopped for a moment to admire his new possession. Jules had constructed a fine home. The stone ends of the structure were carefully and skillfully set with a chimney rising from each. A covered porch across the front of the house shaded it from the morning sun. Shrubs had been planted at each end of the porch and two large maple trees, one on each side, stood at the end of the path leading up to the house. Two outbuildings provided housing for the workers Jules had employed at certain times. Devon smiled to himself that now he would gain the respect he had craved for so long from the other landowners he thought of as lords. He would be one of them now. All he needed to do was present his proof of sale to the governing powers in Newport and begin to enjoy the life he had desired for so long. Tomorrow he would make his way to Newport to register his claim for his new properties.

Devon had come from nothing. His mother had died in one of those illnesses that swept through the colonial frontier every few years. He had been but a boy of eight, living in one of the small settlements along the shore in the north of the great Narragansett Bay, not far from the larger settlement of Providence. His father worked as a horse farrier while his mother kept house and did some baking of fancy goods from time to time. That all changed when his mother had died and his father shortly after took an errant kick from one of the horses he was working on. With both his parents dead within a year, Devon became an orphan with no means. He shifted from one family to another, but knew no affection or kindness, and the length of his stay in any one household was based more on the brutality of his hosts than any measure of affection. Devon had become a loner, surviving despite it all, and grew up to be the mean, clawing individual who envied anyone with possessions and stability. He coveted much and was distrusted and disliked by nearly all. He always felt that others gained what he deserved and never got.

The disappointments in his life had made him hard. He always expected the worst in any situation because that had always been his experience. He had made a good faith offer to buy Jules' holding using the return on future crops as payment. He had no one that would lend him funds. Jules had rejected the offer out of hand, knowing full well that future crops would never be realized. Devon would never make the effort to raise crops. He would sooner hunt and carouse with his cohorts than work. Yet he thought he would become more respected and accepted just by owning a better plot of land.

But tonight would be his last night in his old cabin, perhaps, with the battered stoop at the front door that had to be lifted on its hinges to close tightly, and the creaking floor and fireplace riddled with cracks. It would be the last night of sleeping on the hard bunk of wooden slats with the wind penetrating the cracks in the walls and ill-fitted window. Since Devon had few belongings, it would not take long to move everything to his new residence. After all, it was only a short walk between the two residences: one a ramshackle cabin; the other a well-kept house.

"Where are we going?" Mushqeenupeeash complained as he and Wôquhsak wandered through the woods farther and farther away from the clan's summer camp.

"I do not know, cousin," replied Wôquhsak, "but far enough to keep our loved ones safe."

"Do you have any idea how far that might be, Wôquhsak?" Mushqeenupeeash moaned.

"I think we should try to see the cabin of Devon," Wôquhsak contemplated aloud. "It would not be a bad idea to see the home of Jules, as well."

"But the light is already fading, Wôquhsak, and my feet are tired from carrying this basket," Mushqeenupeeash complained. "Can we not stop for tonight and do this scouting tomorrow?"

Wôquhsak stopped and, in the dimming light, he saw three large standing boulders forming a protective circle in a hollow off to his left.

"We can stop here for tonight," he said to Mushqeenupeeash. "We will need to keep the fire low, but we can bank it near one of the rocks, so we keep as much heat from it as possible."

As the darkness descended and the stars began to appear, the two braves settled down before the fire they had built. Their first night on their own in the woods would be a cold and hungry one, except for some early berries Wôquhsak had come upon. The food their mother had packed for them was going to be kept for the next day since neither of them knew how the hunting might be.

"I am ready to tell you my plan, Mushqeenupeeash," Wôquhsak finally said. "First, I must teach you to whistle."

"I can whistle," Mushqeenupeeash protested. "Perhaps not as well as you, but I can match many of the birds' songs."

"Yes, I know," Wôquhsak said with a slight chuckle, "but this is a different whistle. Did you ever hear the melody that neetôpâwun[152] Jules whistled?"

"I heard it but never thought to copy it," Mushqeenupeeash replied.

"To help make our plan work," Wôquhsak began, "you must learn that song that Jules whistled. And I mean learn it, so it sounds just like it comes from Jules."

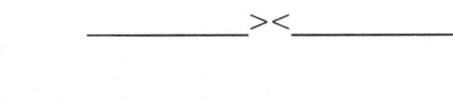

---

[152] Friend

Devon rose before the sun. He was excited by the prospect of being an accepted member of the gentry of the colony. He wanted to get to the trading posts in hopes of catching a small skiff heading to Newport. The day was sunny, and the wind would be calm in the morning.

He dressed in his cleanest waistcoat and the best pair of breeches he owned. He took a rag and tried, as best he could, to put a shine on his boots. He pulled his unkempt hair back and tied it with a small piece of ribbon. He was not sure where the ribbon had come from, but it now served a purpose. Devon reached for his thick leather belt and, almost as an afterthought, took his pistol off the shelf over the fireplace and jammed it into the belt. He donned his battered tricorn and headed out the door.

He pulled the cabin door closed as it made the familiar scraping sound on the uneven floor of the cabin. He scoffed at the sound thinking to himself, "I won't have to hear that much longer." He checked one last time for the paper in his pocket, and satisfied it was there, stepped off the stoop and walked down the short path that led to the Pequot Trail where he would turn north and be at the trading posts at Mill Cove in about an hour's time. This route would take him past the scene of his crime and would give him the opportunity to see if his victim had been discovered. Even if he could not see Jules' body below the trail because it was hidden by the shrubbery, he would certainly hear if it had been found from those at the trading post. It would most likely be the main topic of discussion, a killing of one of them by those murderous savages! He would certainly add to that outrage with his own voice, of course.

Walking confidently along the trail, Devon enjoyed the warmth of the sun and had not a care in the world. His plan was working just as he knew it would. And best of all, someone he felt had always looked down on him and annoyed him with his whistling was gone and would soon be forgotten. For truly, whether his remains were ever found or not, it really mattered little to his plan, because he had proof that he now owned a better property than he had. If Jules' body was found, all the better, for suspicion would be cast on others who were already considered untrustworthy.

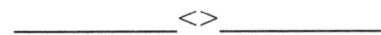

Wôquhsak awoke to the aroma of meat grilling and of someone quietly whistling Jules' tune that he had practiced with Mushqeenupeeash the night before. He sat up and saw Mushqeenupeeash sitting beside the fire roasting a rabbit over the low flame.

"Good morning, cousin," Mushqeenupeeash said brightly. "I caught a rabbit for breakfast. He is not very big, but he will be tasty," he continued.

"When did you wake?" Wôquhsak asked stretching the sleep from his body.

"I did not sleep well," Mushqeenupeeash responded. "That song in my head kept me awake. But I have learned it!" he proudly announced.

"It is good you have learned it," Wôquhsak said with a smile, "for it will be important to my plan."

Mushqeenupeeash removed the broiled carcass of the rabbit from the stick it had been roasted on and offered it to his cousin. Wôquhsak tore a hind leg free and devoured the tender meat from the bone. Mushqeenupeeash smiled at Wôquhsak's hunger. He tore off the remaining hind leg and hungrily began to eat. Neither of them had eaten since morning the day before.

"When we are finished eating," Wôquhsak said as he wiped some juice from his chin, "we will find Devil Devon's cabin and see how it is situated."

Mushqeenupeeash nodded in agreement, and the two finished devouring their breakfast in silence. When they were done, Wôquhsak slipped the quiver of arrows on his back and, taking the bow in his left hand, motioned to Mushqeenupeeash to follow as they left their small camp to find Devon's cabin. Neither of them spoke as they slid through the woods as quietly as possible. Wôquhsak had a general idea of where Devon's cabin stood, but he wanted to see what the surrounding terrain afforded for implementing his plan. Since Sôqanupee had said something about Devon moving, Wôquhsak suspected it might be a move to his victim's home. He and Mushqeenupeeash would still surveil Jules' cabin just so they knew something of the land around it, as well.

Moving with the swiftness and quiet of a forest animal through the pathless undergrowth, Wôquhsak and Mushqeenupeeash quickly crossed the Pequot Trail at a place much further south than where they would have left the trail to reach their clan's summer encampment. They made sure not to be seen crossing the trail and plunged back into the trees on the west side. Keeping a wary eye on their surroundings as they moved between the saplings and large trunks, they soon came to an opening overgrown with weeds and beyond, a small, weathered structure. This was Devon's cabin.

They crouched low at the edge of the field. The fields, the cabin, all looked unkept and abandoned. The field looked untended for more than a year. No smoke curled from the stone chimney of the cabin. There were no signs of anyone being around. Mushqeenupeeash began to rise and Wôquhsak grabbed his forearm and pulled him low again.

"Wait," Wôquhsak cautioned shaking his head. "Look about us before we circle the open area. Look at the trees. Remember the large ones. Which of these might help us in our plan?" Mushqeenupeeash nodded his understanding and began looking at the surrounding land critically. He was not quite sure what he needed to see, but he saw his cousin doing the same thing.

After a few minutes, Wôquhsak began to move along the edge of the clearing. He continued to look at the trees and glancing at the cabin. He seemed to be making mental measurements. Mushqeenupeeash mimicked his movements and began to make his own mental notes. Wôquhsak suddenly stopped and motioned to his cousin to listen.

Mushqeenupeeash crouched motionless and tried to hear what had happened that made Wôquhsak stop, but all he heard was a bird singing. Mushqeenupeeash looked at Wôquhsak with an unspoken question on his face.

"You hear the bird?" Wôquhsak whispered. Mushqeenupeeash nodded, still not understanding.

"The echo!" Wôquhsak whispered excitedly, "it's the echo! Hear it?" he said, pointing at the small bird singing above them, then hearing the echo across the field. Mushqeenupeeash realized what Wôquhsak heard and nodded with a smile.

They continued to move around the edge of the fallow fields until they had reached the north side of the cabin, always looking at the terrain, listening, and watching. They saw much, heard much, and saw no movement about the cabin. Keeping an eye on the path that led from the Pequot Trail up to the cabin, the two braves quietly crept up to the side of the cabin. Wôquhsak pressed his ear against the wall of the cabin and listened for any movement from within. Nothing. He carefully rose against the wall to reach the level of the window in the wall. He peeked through the dirty pane of glass and saw no one.

He tapped Mushqeenupeeash on the shoulder and the two moved as shadows around the corner of the cabin to the cabin door. Wôquhsak tried the latch handle; the door gave slightly and stuck at its foot. He gave it a slightly stronger push and it opened. There was no movement within.

Mushqeenupeeash and Wôquhsak quickly entered the small cabin and looked to see if any items were present that would indicate someone was living there. They saw enough to know that someone had recently been in the residence. Knowing this, they left all as they had found it and quickly exited, pulling the door closed until the latch securely dropped. They slipped off the stoop and rounded the north corner of the cabin and, keeping low, crossed the weed-infested field to the north and slid into the woods beyond.

EIGHT

DEVON HAD REACHED THE TRADING POSTS ON MILL cove just in time to catch a small shallop about to cast off for the sail across the bay to Newport. He grudgingly bartered a copper coin for his passage and found himself a place along the port railing where he could sit out of the wind and out of the way. Besides, he had other things that concerned him.

When he passed the site of the murder he had committed two days before, there was no sign of the war club he had purposely left in sight on the trail. The place where he had shoved the body off the trail and down the embankment toward the cove was so thickly filled with ground cover, he could not tell if the body of Jules was still there or if it had been discovered and removed. He expected to hear talk among the men at the trading post of a body being discovered, yet nothing had been said. There had certainly been people traveling on the Pequot Trail. Had someone picked up the war club without questioning why it was lying on the trail? Did they not notice the blood on it?

What puzzled him more than anything else was when he checked to see that the hat and cloak were still hidden in the crevasse of the rock on the other side of the trail, he discovered they were gone. Because he spent so much time at the murder site, he was late getting to the trading posts and nearly missed his transport to Newport. He had not had a great amount of time to see if there was any talk of Jules' demise and if his body had been discovered, although he would have expected that would be the most important news. And now, he was lost in these thoughts as the sailboat rounded the point into the great Narragansett Bay.

Wôquhsak and Mushqeenupeeash crouched at the edge of the field south of Jules' cabin. They knew this cabin well having been there several times when Jules welcomed his native friends. The field before them was neatly planted. The first signs of various plants were just breaking through the weed-free dirt of the neat rows. They looked for signs of activity in the cabin. All was quiet. The two braves, staying low, circled the cabin at a distance and listened for places that returned echoes. When they were satisfied that no one was about, they slowly crept closer.

They made note of the front porch with its covering roof. The ends of the porch were not finished with a vertical board, so the underside of the porch was open. Along the front there was a few inches clearance between the face board of the porch and the ground. Wôquhsak stood looking at the trees about the property. There were two large maple trees, one on either side at the start of the path leading up to the cabin from the Pequot Trail. Another large elm tree stood at the end of the tree line where the Pequot Trail disappeared into forest again beyond the open field south of the cabin.

"No one is here," Mushqeenupeeash whispered to his cousin. "I do not like this."

"It is odd," Wôquhsak replied in the same whispered tone. "Devon is not at his cabin and is not here. We will need to watch both until we see him. We will have time to set out our plan but, for now, let us go back to our camp and be patient."

Wôquhsak and Mushqeenupeeash bent low as they loped through the open field and slid silently into the forest to the south of the cabin. Once in the safety of the undergrowth and trees, the braves made their way back to their temporary camp among the large boulders. Along the way, they might find some game larger than a rabbit for their arrows.

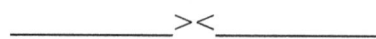

Devon had enjoyed his night on the town in the city of Newport. It was rare for him to make the trip across the bay. He hated the city with its noise and people. He had spent most of the day after his arrival at the colonial offices filing his claim to the lands and homestead of Jules de Vendome. He presented his paper indicating what he purported to be the mark of his victim along with the bloody fingerprint to the colonial officials. He was not expecting the reaction he received upon telling his story of Jules' sudden departure from the area.

Jules was well known in the colonial office. He had said nothing to anyone there about receiving word of his being needed at home. In fact, most of the colonial office felt Jules had become a permanent resident. There was skepticism expressed since no one had heard of his leaving. But news was slow to arrive and sometimes lost in transit in the new colonies, and Devon's insistence that Jules had received word from home was not out of the realm of possibility. He insisted that the colonial record be checked and, until he was proven wrong then, his claim be approved. And so, it was resolved for now.

With his success at the land offices, Devon retired to one of the waterfront bars and proceeded to celebrate and be feted by his fellow bar flies for his good fortune, not that any one of them really cared, just as long as someone else was paying for their rum. And that explained his awakening the next morning with a splitting headache, wrapped in an old piece of canvas in the alley behind the bar, with not so much as a farthing left in his pocket. At that moment, he was glad he had already paid his fare to the captain of the boat he had taken to Newport the day before. Now he knew he needed to get back to the dock before it sailed back across the bay without him. The captain would not delay sailing to wait for him.

Mushqeenupeeash checked his snares on the way back to camp hoping to find another catch. Wôquhsak had gone on to their camp. Mushqeenupeeash enjoyed hunting and being on his own in the forest. He was at ease with nature, but he was not so with Wôquhsak's plan. He was uneasy with the idea that they could make a wôpusu[153] admit what he had done to one of his own kind. How could a whistled tune and the victim's cloak and hat make this happen? His thoughts were interrupted by finding a small squirrel in one of his snares. It might not be much, but it would do for a small meal for both him and his cousin.

Wôquhsak restoked the small fire at camp. While he waited for Mushqeenupeeash to return to their temporary camp, he set about clearing the leaves and twigs from a two-foot square patch of the forest ground sheltered by the boulders. He then began to use some of the twigs to make a crude map to represent Jules' cabin and the surrounding fields. He marked the areas where he and Mushqeenupeeash had noted echoes were strongest. He took a few pine twigs and used them to identify the large trees of which they had made note. Next, he gathered some small stones from nearby soil and lined out the fields and the rock walls that lined the path leading to the cabin and ran along the Pequot Trail defining the fields to the south of the cabin.

He sat back and was admiring his work when Mushqeenupeeash came into camp with his prizes from the snares. He held up a squirrel and a rabbit with a smile of success on his face. Then he noticed the cleared patch of ground and the rough plan sketched out upon it.

---

[153] White Man

"Do you recognize this?" Wôquhsak asked him.

"It is Jules' cabin and fields, is it not?" Mushqeenupeeash responded.

It is," Wôquhsak replied smiling, "and it is how we will make Devon admit his crime." Mushqeenupeeash nodded, not yet fully grasping how Wôquhsak's plan would work.

As they roasted the small catch above the fire, Wôquhsak went about explaining to Mushqeenupeeash how his plan would unfold. But for the next few days, they would need to scout each location until they saw activity and knew that Devon was back. Wôquhsak was hopeful that, by the time they began to implement his plan, they would have the original pahqumuhq[154] back from Crow, their weapon maker, along with the additional ones he had created.

After they had picked the charred carcasses of all their meat, they sat together in front of the design Wôquhsak had created on the cleared patch of forest ground. Wôquhsak carefully showed Mushqeenupeeash the locations he felt they could use to institute his plan.

"As soon as we know where Devon will be living, we can begin to devil him," Wôquhsak said after. "I am hoping he will choose to live in the cabin of Jules. I must think that is the only reason he would do what he has done."

"How long do you think it will take before Devon breaks?" Mushqeenupeeash asked.

"If we are patient and clever, and he believes strongly in the spirits and the great Manutoo[155], as we have been led to believe he does, it could be quicker than you might think," Wôquhsak replied. "We must wait until we know he has returned. It cannot be much longer until the body of Jules is found."

"Is that important to your plan?" Mushqeenupeeash questioned.

---

[154] Narragansett war club. Literally, 'head splitter'
[155] Spirit / Creator

"It would only make time more important," Wôquhsak answered. "Once the body is found, the wôpusuwak[156] will begin to search for his killer in earnest. They will send out armed searchers and begin pillaging our villages. We will need then to put more pressure on Devon if he has resisted our efforts." Mushqeenupeeash nodded in agreement.

Wôquhsak knew they would need to be patient until they saw Devon return. Before then, they would scout Devon's dilapidated cabin and Jules' stone-ended cabin twice a day until they were sure he had returned. Until then, he and his cousin would hunt for small game and set their snares for food and try to be comfortable in their temporary camp. Wôquhsak and Mushqeenupeeash continued to whistle softly and hum the song of Jules even playing a bit with one of them starting and the other starting after. They had sometimes heard the wôpusuwak[157] do this with songs when they had much drink or in what some called their "church."

Each day, Wôquhsak checked the basket containing the precious cloak and hat of their friend Jules. He made sure they were dry and did not show any creases from the folding. He took them out and folded them differently to keep them neat. He tried to avoid touching the bloodstain on the collar, now a dried brown blot against the reddish hue of the cloak. Wôquhsak carefully placed the hat on top of the cloak with one side of its brim folded up and the other turned down just as its owner had worn it. His thoughts turned to the pahqumuhq[158] left with his clan's weapons maker, Crow. Would he have the war club replicated in time? He could only hope.

---

156 White Men
157 Ibid Footnote 156
158 Narragansett war club. Literally, 'head splitter'

NINE

THE BOAT CARRYING DEVON ROUNDED THE POINT INTO Mill Cove and slackened its sails as it approached Smith's trading post. Devon roused himself as the level of activity and noise rose aboard the shallop. He had slept most of the way from Newport in his spot along the railing, undisturbed and ignored by the crew. The pounding in his head from his drinking the night before had lessened only slightly.

The shore seemed strangely quiet. He had expected by now there would be some commotion and excited talk about a body being discovered; the head wound obviously caused by some savage's war club for reasons unknown. Perhaps, it was robbery, or just because these natives sometimes killed for no reason. After all, they were savages! But Devon saw no gathering of outraged men; no voices demanding vengeance. Nothing.

He gathered his shoulder pouch and hat and stepped up over the railing onto the dock. Confused by the calm of all around him, Devon slowly walked down the dock to the porch of the trading post. He was greeted there by Mr. Wilcox seated in his usual rocking chair just beside the door under the shade of the porch.

"Been to town, I see," Wilcox intoned with a slight bit of sarcasm. "Looks like ye had a good night." Devon ignored the sarcastic tone.

"Know of anyone heading south on the trail?" Devon asked.

Wilcox leaned forward in his chair and spat some tobacco juice on the ground, then turned to his left and shouted in his graveled voice to unseen figures inside the trading post, "Anybody goin' south on the trail?"

The low rumble of voices coming from inside the doorway suddenly subsided and a form appeared through the door.

"I'm headin' south, Boss," a short man dressed in deerskin leggings, linen shirt, and a dirty and ragged green woolen short jacket with brass buttons replied. "Who wants to know?" he continued.

"Name's Devon," came the reply from Devon. "If yer headin' south on the trail, I'm headin' that way, as well. Mind if we travel together?"

"Lemme grab my pack. My names Barker, by the way," the man replied and hurried back inside the trading post.

In a few moments, he reappeared with a large bundle wrapped in deerskin and tied with rawhide straps slung over his shoulder, and a long-barreled musket in his right hand. On his head he now wore a brimmed hat that had seen better days. With his long hair pulled back under the hat, Devon was able to see where the man's ear should have been, there was nothing but a poorly healed scar.

Devon shouldered his own bag and the two headed down the short path that led to the Pequot Trail. As Barker attempted to make some conversation, Devon was deep in thought about how he was going to make sure the body of Jules de Vendome was going to be discovered. And the discoverer was expounding away as he walked along next to him.

They reached the trail as Barker was relating to Devon how he was just passing through this part of the colony on his way to better hunting he had heard about from another trapper in the colony of Pennsylvania. His pack held some trinkets and trade goods he could use along the way to obtain food from tribes if they were friendly. Even better, Devon thought to himself. This person would not know who the body he was about to discover was, nor would he know its relationship with his walking companion. It was perfect.

As they walked along the trail, Devon began listening to what Barker was saying with more interest and began actively conversing.

"Where are you coming from?" Devon asked his gabby friend when he could finally get a word in.

"I've been up north in the lakes by the White Mountains. Pretty up there," Barker observed. "That area seems all but trapped out for good pelts. But I hear western part of Pennsylvania is rich in game, so I'm headin' there."

They were getting close to the spot where Devon had committed his gruesome act. Suddenly, Devon stopped and put his arm out in front of his walking companion.

"What has happened here?" Devon said inspecting the ground with his eyes feigning discovery. "Something happened here." His companion dropped his pack and bent close to the ground.

"Aye," he said in a muffled voice. "There are tracks here that someone tried to wipe away. Boots and moccasins. There's blood here, as well." Devon stood silently as Barker used his tracking skill to uncover all he could.

"It looks like someone was injured here," Devon finally said softly.

"There's more," Barker said following marks all but invisible to the untrained eye. "See these drag marks? Something was dragged off the trail into the bushes." Barker began to follow the marks toward the bushes when he suddenly stopped in mid-step.

"Smell that?" he asked, turning to look at Devon who had moved behind him.

"Aye," came Devon's reply.

"That's the smell of somethin' rotting," Barker said with gravity in his voice. "Somethin's dead in them bushes."

"Or," suggested Devon, "someone?"

Cautiously pulling some of the underbrush branches aside, Barker confirmed it was a body. Devon tried his best to be surprised.

"We should not touch it," Devon suggested. "We need to have others see it before we move it. I'll wait here while you go back to the trading post and bring some help. Bring a blanket or something to wrap the body in."

"Are ya' sure?" came the reply from Barker.

"I am," Devon said sternly. "Leave yer pack here. You'll be quicker without carrying it." Barker nodded agreement and ran back up the trail with his rifle still in his hand.

As soon as Barker was out of sight, Devon began looking around for the war club he had used to bludgeon Jules. He could not find it anywhere. He could not remember if he had pushed it to the side of the trail or pushed it into the bushes alongside the trail. He went across to the west side of the clearing thinking he had tossed it there. Nothing. No war club anywhere. He went to the crevasse in the rock outcrop where he had hidden the cloak and hat of his victim. They too were still missing. He was looking among the low shrubs when the sounds of men approaching forced him to stop. Four men were hurrying down the trail from the direction of the trading posts with Barker in the lead. Devon recognized one of them as Mr. Wilcox's assistant. He knew the others, as well.

"It's over here," Barker was saying as he pointed in the direction of the putrid odor.

"What are you doin' 'ere, Devon?" Wilcox's assistant said, eyeing Devon head to toe.

"I just got back from Newport and was headed home," Devon replied.

"Mr. Devon and I were traveling together," Barker cut in. "We found the body together." He wanted his share of the credit

As they spoke, the other three men had retrieved the lifeless corpse of Jules de Vendome from among the bushes and were gingerly placing it in the blanket one of them had been carrying. Each of them had covered their noses with cloth.

"It's Jules," one of the men said. "Looks like he was clubbed on the head."

Devon was about to speak when Barker blurted out what Devon was about to say.

"Probably some savage wantin' to rob him," Barker offered.

"Look for a weapon," Wilcox's assistant ordered.

"That is what I was doing when you arrived," Devon said. "Didn't find one."

"The killer wouldn't have left it," another of the men offered up.

"Mr. Wilcox said to bring the body back to the trading post and both of you, as well," the leader said.

"I just got back from Newport," Devon began to complain.

"Good fer you," the leader answered. "You can rest at the trading post. Now, pick up a corner of that blanket and let's get back to the post before the sun gets any higher and the day gets hotter."

TEN

FOR THREE DAYS AND NIGHTS, WÔQUHSAK AND MUSH-qeenupeeash faithfully scouted Devon's ramshackle cabin and Jules' well-maintained home. Finding no sign of Devon, Wôquhsak was beginning to think his plan was unworkable. Everything had been planned, and all the signs of success were there. The three-quarter moon was waxing toward full; the weather was holding warm and clear. The first full moon of early summer would shine brightly. Only the pahqumuhq[159] being made by the weapon maker, Kôkôch (Crow), were not in hand, but would be soon. Everything was ready but the target of the plan was nowhere to be found. Wôquhsak was fearing they might have to abandon the plan if Devon did not appear soon. He would give it one more day before he decided what to do.

They had made their morning and evening scouts of both cabins and were returning to camp for a fourth day, deflated. Still no sign of Devon. As they slid between the rocks that formed the den of their camp, there, on the rocks next to the fire were three identical pahqumuhq[160]. Wôquhsak drew his hunting knife, unsure of how these war clubs had arrived at their camp. From behind him, he suddenly heard a familiar voice.

---

[159] Narragansett war club (plural). Literally 'head splitter'
[160] Ibid Footnote 159

"Is this how I taught you to conceal a camp," the voice said. It was a voice both Wôquhsak and Mushqeenupeeash recognized. It was Nuhshwanum Nâhneepawuhshat (three Dog Moon), Wôquhsak's father.

"How did you find us?" Wôquhsak said, racing into his father's arms. "We knew someone was here because we saw the pahqumuhq[161] by the fire."

"You left enough of a trail that a blind man could have found his way here," Nuhshwanum Nâhneepawuhshat replied laughing slightly. He nodded and smiled at Mushqeenupeeash who stood on the other side of the fire.

The three of them sat around the small fire and examined the three war clubs Wôquhsak's father had brought to the camp. Each was identical to the others. Crow, the weapon maker, had even dipped each of the rock balls forming the heads in blood and let it dry.

"Tell me what this plan of yours is to trick Devon into confessing," Nuhshwanum Nâhneepawuhshat began. "I heard from your mother what little she knew, and I talked with the Elders, but they knew little more. What is this plan to avenge our neetôpâwun[162] Jules de Vendome?"

"I want Devon to grow afraid that the great Manutoo[163] is angry with him for killing our friend," Wôquhsak related to his father. "I want to haunt him into confessing to his fellow wôpusuwak[164] what he did so they will not blame our people."

"What can I do to help you?" his father asked.

"Do you remember the song neetôpâwun[165] Jules whistled all the time?" Wôquhsak asked.

---

[161] Narragansett war club. (plural) Literally, 'head splitters'
[162] Friend
[163] Spirit
[164] White Men
[165] Friend

"Some of it, but it was a simple tune I am sure I can learn quickly," his father replied.

"Then we will be ready to begin my plan as soon as we know Devon has returned," Wôquhsak said staring into the fire.

"What do you mean?" Wôquhsak's father asked. "I have heard the body of Jules had been found three days ago. The wôpusuwak[166] will begin entering our villages any day now. We must employ your plan quickly!"

"We do not know where Devon is, Uncle," Mushqeenupeeash responded. He had been listening intently and wanted to be part of the conversation.

"What Mushqeenupeeash says is the truth, Father," Wôquhsak continued. "We have been watching for him where we think he should be but have had no sign of him."

"We are afraid he has gone away and will not return," Mushqeenupeeash said in a disappointed voice.

"He will return, my sons," Nuhshwanum Nâhneepawuhshat said with surety. "He killed for a reason, the reason of jealousy. He wanted to possess what our friend Jules had worked hard to have. But Devon would never work that hard to have the same. He will return."

"And we will be ready when he does," Wôquhsak said confidently.

The sky was darkening, and the glow of the fire lit the small group among the boulders.

Nuhshwanum Nâhneepawuhshat, named for the three Dogs who were howling at the moon the night he was born, had brought some fish with him freshly caught that morning from the summer camp. As he laid the filets above the fire, he made sure the boys knew their mother, Upeeshâwônkoon, had lovingly cleaned and prepared this meal for them.

Wôquhsak did not sleep well that night. He had not told his father that the next day would be the fourth without knowing Devon's

---

166 White Men

79

whereabouts. But his father's news of the discovery of Jules' body made the decision he thought he would need to make unnecessary. Now other events he could not control were in motion that he had hoped to delay as long as possible. Soon the wôpusuwak[167] would be marching into the camps of his people and rummaging through their huts and mistreating people. These were things he had hoped to avoid, but his plan to do so was taking too long to implement. He could only hope Devon would appear soon.

Devon's decision to try to speed up the discovery of Jules de Vendome's body had wound up costing him four days and another voyage across the bay to Newport. The colonial authorities there had sent word to Providence for Roger Williams, himself, to investigate the atrocity. It had taken a full day for him to arrive from Providence. It was only after he arrived that everyone became aware that the victim was an acquaintance of Roger Williams. Several officials questioned Devon and Barker repeatedly about their discovery. When was the last time the victim had been seen alive? Was any weapon found? Did they know the deceased? Did they know anyone who might have had a grudge or disagreement with the victim? Since Barker was not even from the area, it fell to Devon to answer most of these questions. He had lied where he needed to and made unfounded suggestions regarding the suspected killer when needed.

The other men who had been present when the body was recovered were questioned in the same manner. Devon's attempts while crossing the bay to firmly plant into every member's mind the idea of the perpetrator being a rogue native using a war club was repeated as fact by every testimony. It was just by luck that no mention was made of the recent acquisition of the assets of the decedent by one of those

---

[167] White Men

testifying, a fact that might have placed suspicion squarely on one of those present. The only other benefit Devon derived during his enforced stay was being lodged and fed at the expense of the colonial government since he had no money. It was a benefit also enjoyed by Barker.

The inquiry finally decided on the afternoon of the third day that the unfortunate demise of this respected individual was by hands of an unknown person or persons of the native population. The matter would continue to be investigated under the direction of Roger Williams with whatever assistance he required from the authorities.

Barker, Devon, and the rest of the witnesses were free to go with the thanks of the colonial officers for their statements. While Devon and the other men would leave the next morning for Mill Cove and home, Barker had decided he would find a ship going west to the New York or New Jersey colony and make his way to Pennsylvania from there. As a form of compensation from the Inquiry Board, Barker's travel expense was paid and Devon's was, likewise, compensated. Knowing that Barker would likely never be seen in the colony again, Devon felt a certain level of security about the testimony he had manufactured.

ELEVEN

THE SUN ROSE IN A CLOUDLESS SKY AND PROMISED A warm day. Wôquhsak [168] sat with his father and showed him the plan he had laid out on the ground for Mushqeenupeeash[169]. Mushqeenupeeash was on the morning scout of the cabins and would check his snares on the way back to the camp. Wôquhsak and his father were practicing whistling Jules' melody when Mushqeenupeeash came into camp with two fat rabbits in hand. Absent-mindedly, Mushqeenupeeash joined in. As he expertly skinned and prepared the rabbits for roasting, the three of them sat around the fire whistling the simple tune.

Mushqeenupeeash reported nothing had changed at either of the locations scouted. Wôquhsak was becoming concerned that there might be no way to stop the wôpusuwak[170] from invading the camps of his people and taking revenge for a murder they were innocent of having committed. Since the body of Jules had been recovered and the cause of his death was surely to be blamed on the native population, Wôquhsak knew his plan must start soon if it was to achieve its goal of having the real murderer confess.

---

[168] Five Foxes
[169] Red River
[170] White Men

During the day, the three talked about the plan. Wôquhsak told his father every detail, reviewing every step as they escalated the pressure on Devon. All they needed was for him to return and they would then know how quickly the plan would need to play out. They talked of Jules and his kindness toward, not just their clan, but the entire Narragansett tribe. For all of that, they would avenge his death.

As the sun began to set, Mushqeenupeeash left Wôquhsak and Nuhshwanum Nâhneepawuhshat at camp and went to scout and check his snares, as usual. He was hoping to find his snares had met with success. He was not so hopeful about seeing any change in the cabins he scouted.

While he was gone, his companions back at camp went about gathering wood for the fire and retrieving water from the small stream that ran nearby to camp. The fire would be ready for Mushqeenupeeash's return and hoped for success of his snares. After doing their tasks, Nuhshwanum Nâhneepawuhshat began telling his son about his hunt that he had returned from only to find his son gone. It had been a successful hunt. Three deer had been killed, and they would feed the clan for some time to come.

Suddenly, Mushqeenupeeash appeared in the space between two of the boulders shielding the camp. He was out of breath from running and needed a moment before he could speak. But the look on his face said something his words would only confirm.

"He's back!" he almost shouted. "I saw him in his cabin. He was leaving with a bundle on his back. He was leaving with everything he owned!"

"I think he is going to Jules' cabin," Wôquhsak said.

Forgetting about food, Wôquhsak, Nuhshwanum Nâhneepawuhshat, and Mushqeenupeeash left the fire and slipped into the trees onto the path that would lead them to Jules' cabin. They moved with cautious speed, making as little noise as possible, the light from the setting sun allowing them to see their way through the trees and bushes. Wôquhsak could feel his heart racing.

_____><_____

Devon pushed open the door to his cabin and looked about. It would be the last time he would survey its drab, dirty interior. Even so, he was happy to be back on the west side of the bay and away from the people and noise of the city. Three days had been enough. Now, all he needed to do was gather his few clothes and the few other possessions he had and close the door to what he saw as his past life. He would find someone else to live here - for a fee, of course.

As he strolled down the path from his cabin to the Pequot Trail, Devon had a feeling of accomplishment. He had eliminated someone he disliked, even hated for his ease of personality, a friend to all, liked by everyone. He now held all that person's possessions. And all had been accomplished without anyone being aware of his involvement in making it come about. He could hardly stand his own cleverness. At this point, who was there to contest his new possessions? Certainly not the last owner whose signature and thumbprint were affixed to a bill of sale. Oh, did I forget to mention how cleverly Devon had copied the signature of his victim from a note at the trading post from a receipt for a purchase Jules had made?

And now, he was on his way to taking possession of his ill-gotten gains. He could not help but smile to himself. So, with his clothes and few possessions wrapped in a blanket from his bed slung over his shoulder, his ancient pistol in his belt, and his smooth-bore rifle in his left hand, Devon strolled down the trail heading for his new home unaware of the eyes watching him..

Devon lifted the latch to his new home and slowly pushed open the cabin door. It was clean. It was attractive and everything was put on shelves built into the walls. It was organized as if a woman's hand had been used. Devon's first thought was for food. He had not eaten for most of the day. He went to a door by the table in what passed for a kitchen and found it was the larder. He found some dried sausage and a bottle of wine. A crust of bread only a few days old and still soft enough to eat completed his first meal in his new cabin.

After he had satisfied his hunger and finished the bottle of wine, Devon decided to search for anything of value. He began ransacking every inch of the cabin. There were only a few places he thought Jules would have hidden things like his money or other valuables. His search got him nothing more than a cabin that now showed the disorganization of a ransacking. A chest that had stood against one wall was thrown open and its contents strewn about. The small closet in the bedroom now had clothes tossed on the floor. Devon's efforts yielded nothing.

He sat on the bed exhausted. It had been a long day, and the bed felt softer than his old one and called him to sleep. As he stripped off his boots and dropped them to the floor, one boot landed with a distinctly different sound than the other. Devon looked at the floor where his boots now lay. The board beneath the boot that had made a hollow sound looked as if it would lift easily. Devon pulled his knife from the sheath on his belt and carefully guided the blade into the space next to the floorboard. The board easily lifted, and he deftly slid the fingers of his left hand under the edge.

Beneath the board was a small rectangular space containing a small rectangular box, its lid held closed by a small latch. Devon lifted the box and flipped the latch on the cover. There it was. A gold ring and a gold crucifix glittered before his eyes. Next to them was a small leather pouch. Devon picked up the pouch and realized it was larger than what it first appeared. He bounced it in the air against his open palm and heard the clink of coins. He turned to his right and poured the contents of the pouch on the cover of the bed. The coins rang against each other as they tumbled onto the bed. There were more coins than Devon had ever seen in his life. Some he recognized; others he did not. But he knew they were all valuable and would easily buy him all the food and drink he could desire. Tomorrow he would go to the trading post.

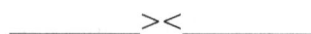

Wôquhsak, and his two companions arrived at the edge of the woods bordering the planted field south of Jules' cabin. The moon was rising as the last rays of sunlight faded in the west. Smoke was curling up into the sky from the chimney of the cabin and a dim light was visible through the window that faced them. Someone was in residence, and all knew it was not Jules de Vendome. Wôquhsak tapped his cousin and father on their shoulders and pointed back into the woods. He wanted to leave before they could be discovered. Now they knew Devon was back and had moved into Jules' cabin, Wôquhsak could begin his plan the next night.

TWELVE

IT WAS DARK BY THE TIME THE TRIO OF WÔQUHSAK, Mushqeenupeeash and Nuhshwanum Nâhneepawuhshat got back to their camp. Mushqeenupeeash went to gather more wood for the fire while Wôquhsak prepared the snared catch for dinner that had been dropped and forgotten when Mushqeenupeeash raced into camp with his news of Devon. Wôquhsak's father inspected the three war clubs that sat next to the basket containing the hat and cloak of Jules.

"These pahqumuhq[171] cannot be seen to be different," Nuhshwanum Nâhneepawuhshat said as he turned them over and over looking at them intently.

"That is good, Father," Wôquhsak said, laying more wood on the fire. "They will play a large part in my plan."

Mushqeenupeeash returned to the firelight with an armful of twigs and small branches. It only took a few minutes to roast the fat rabbit Mushqeenupeeash's snare had caught and satisfied the hunger gnawing at the stomachs of the three who consumed it. Wôquhsak wanted to be sure of Devon's movements, and so he wanted to keep an eye on him through the night and into the next day. His father suggested that Devon would not leave at this late hour and there was no need to

---

[171] Narragansett war club. (plural) Literally 'head splitter'

watch him through the night. Morning would be the earliest he might leave. If one of them were observing before sunrise, they would know if Devon left. Wôquhsak agreed and the three of them bedded down on the ground to sleep.

An hour before the sun rose, Wôquhsak was on the path leading to the cabin of Jules. He quietly settled in the same place at the edge of the woods by the south field they had been using to watch the cabin. It was a cool morning with only the birds breaking the silence of the scene. Wôquhsak was anxious to put his plan into action. Moonrise tonight would be perfect if the weather held, and the few clouds floating high in the sky certainly looked promising.

It was not long before Wôquhsak saw a slight curl of smoke appear above the chimney of the cabin. Wôquhsak pulled his deerskin wrap a bit tighter against the cool morning air. The sun was fully up when Wôquhsak saw Devon as he left the cabin with his musket in hand and headed north on the Pequot Trail. His pace was a fast walk, and he seemed to have confidence in his step as he walked with his gun over his shoulder. Wôquhsak did not know where Devon was going but he did not think it was far because he had taken only his musket. Wôquhsak suspected he would return before dark. His plan would begin tonight.

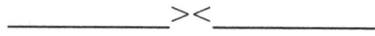

Devon was enjoying the warm air as he walked along the well-worn Pequot Trail toward the trading posts on Mill Cove. In the small pouch inside his deerskin bag tied to his belt he could feel the weight of the coins he had found in the cabin. He had plans to celebrate the success of his scheme. He had no real friends so he would celebrate alone with as much whiskey as he could buy at the trading posts.

Devon was feeling confident and, for the first time in as long as he could remember, happy. Everything he had wanted had come to him and, best of all, he was above suspicion. What did it matter to him if a few of the native population would suffer for the act he had committed? Sooner or later, the bloodlust for revenge would pass and all would return to the uneasy peace that had existed before the death of Jules de Vendome. It was none of his concern in any event.

As Devon turned off the Pequot Trail onto the path leading to the trading posts on Mill Cove, he could only think about how much whiskey he might be able to carry.

Wôquhsak had watched Devon disappear up the Pequot Trail. He had risen from his sitting position and turned to head back to his camp. He expected his companions would be up by now and wondering when Devon might return. There was much to do in preparation before night came. The first part of Wôquhsak's plan required knowing when Devon returned. They would only know that if they kept watch for him. That might require several trips to Jules' cabin throughout the day.

When Wôquhsak entered the camp, Mushqeenupeeash was sitting next to the fire with Wôquhsak's father eating some of the food given to them by Wôquhsak's mother. Mushqeenupeeash offered some to his cousin with a smile.

"Devon has left to go somewhere," Wôquhsak announced showing little concern. "I feel he will return before nightfall, so we must be ready."

Wôquhsak set aside two of the war clubs and explained how he wanted to use them that night. He carefully unfolded Jules' cloak and the hat from the basket and laid them on the ground. He and Mushqeenupeeash began gathering vines from around the camp while his father started cutting branches from young pine trees. Together, they fashioned a skeleton of branches lashed together with vines that fit inside the cloak. An extension of a branch extended at the neck that fit inside the hat.

The cloak hung about six inches above the ground and a tripod of larger branches lashed strongly together allowed the structure to stand on its own. The three of them stood back to admire their work. Standing near it, anyone would know it was not a person. But, from a distance, it would pass for a standing figure. The pine needles of the branches put pressure on the cloak and made it fill out as would a body. The hat left a shaded place where a face might be and drooped on the down-turned side to meet the cloak. Wôquhsak was sure it would serve its purpose.

Wôquhsak, Mushqeenupeeash, and Nuhshwanum Nâhneepawuhshat spent the rest of the afternoon softly whistling Jules' melody. It was now owned by them, as well. They rested and talked about the events about to occur and the results they hoped they would foster. Every couple of hours, one of the three would make their way to the edge of the south field at Jules' cabin to see if Devon had returned. As the sun moved westward in the sky, and there was no sign of Devon, Wôquhsak began to worry that all their preparations might be in vain. Nuhshwanum Nâhneepawuhshat's return from his second trip to the cabin brought the welcome news that Devon had returned.

Devon had wiled away the entire day at the Smith trading post on Mill Cove. He had listened to the heated debate regarding the killing of Jules de Vendome. Many of those at the trading post were in favor of joining the armed men expected to arrive any day from Newport or Providence to begin punishing the native population for this act against the white settlers. The few who spoke against quick action were roundly shouted down and called cowardly. All Devon knew was someone kept his glass of whiskey full as he happily added more fuel to the fiery debate.

Devon had purchased two small kegs of the best whiskey Wilcox had for sale. The only admonishment from Wilcox being not to share any drink with the natives. Devon laughed at the suggestion. The kegs were heavy, and Devon needed to improvise to get them back home. He asked for a length of rope from a pile of discarded cordage in the corner of the trading post. He found a couple of lengths of siding that had been replaced on the building. They were rotted, but not completely. Devon used the rope to tie these planks to two small tree branches to form a kind of sledge. Placing the two casks on the structure and using another rope to secure them, he could pull the casks with some ease.

Devon had done this when he first arrived at the trading post. And it was a good thing he had. By the time he was ready to leave, his consumption of whiskey would have made it nearly impossible for him to construct his sledge. With a final wave of his hand and a slurred "farewell," Devon had headed for home. Several of those who had been drinking with him noted a definite sway in his step as he dragged the sledge behind him up the path to the Pequot Trail.

><

Wôquhsak and Nuhshwanum Nâhneepawuhshat sat quietly at the edge of the south field watching Devon sitting on the porch of Jules' cabin.

"Something is wrong with him," Wôquhsak whispered to his father.

"He has been drinking the strong water of the Whites," Nuhshwanum Nâhneepawuhshat replied. "This is good for your plan."

"How is this good?" Wôquhsak asked, confused at his father's statement.

"The strong water makes the Whites more susceptible to things they think they hear and see," his father answered. "It is a good thing for your plan."

They watched Devon for a few more minutes as he sat on the porch resting a foot on one cask and cradling the other under his arm. They could hear him attempting to carry a melody, but it was easy to tell he had no voice for singing. Yet, he continued, blissfully unaware of being watched. When they had seen and heard enough, Wôquhsak and his father slipped back into the trees and headed back to camp.

"Only a few more hours and the moon will be high, and we can begin," Wôquhsak thought to himself.

Wôquhsak increased his pace as he neared their camp. His father lagged, but Wôquhsak wanted to share the news with Mushqeenupeeash. Nuhshwanum Nâhneepawuhshat arrived at the camp to see a flurry of activity as his son began gathering two of the pahqumuhq[172] and the scarecrow wearing the cloak and hat.

"Calm, my son," Nuhshwanum Nâhneepawuhshat caught his son by the shoulder. "There is plenty of time and calmer heads make better decisions." Wôquhsak nodded in understanding.

For the last time, Wôquhsak reviewed with his comrades what their assignments were. He would initiate each phase of the plan, and they would know when to follow with their part. All they could do for now was wait and watch the moon rise above the trees into the night sky with only a few clouds.

---

[172] Narragansett war club. Literally 'head splitter'

THIRTEEN

DEVON WAS DEEP INTO HIS FIRST CASK OF WHISKEY AS he sat on the porch bench with it next to him. He could not remember a day in his life when he had had so much to drink, first at the trading post and now on the porch of his newly acquired cabin. He had sung every song he knew in his raspy croak and watched the sky darken and the moon rise. The stars were little pinpricks of blurred light in his stupor. But it was pleasant sitting there in the cool of an early summer evening with a rising moon, plenty of drink, and dulled senses.

Suddenly, very faintly, Devon became aware of a sound. His dulled senses could not immediately identify what it was, but he knew it was familiar. As his mind cleared a bit from the fog of drink, he heard it again. He thought to himself, "is that a bird?" No, no. It wasn't a bird. It was someone or something whistling! Whistling a melody he instantly recognized! But that was impossible! Jules was dead!

And there it was again, but not from the same direction. It was from his left where it had been on his right. He was sure it had come from his right. And now again! This time from behind the cabin! Now again from the right. Now from both sides. Devon thought his ears were playing tricks on him. He stuck a whiskey-soaked finger in his ear and shook it trying to stop the sound.

Then silence. Only the normal evening sounds of the nocturnal animals. Devon stuck the pinkie of his left hand into his left ear again and rapidly moved it about before removing it. Then he listened again. Just the night sounds. He decided he was just hearing things because of the drink. But then, it was there again, resounding from every direction, louder than ever. He tried to stand and realized he needed to lean against the cabin wall for support. The cacophony of whistling was deafening! He was more unsteady on his feet than he had thought. With both hands he lifted the cask, which was much lighter than when he had set it down and, tucking it under one arm, he pushed open the cabin door with his shoulder and stumbled into the cabin kicking the full cask through the door with his foot.

He had barely set the cask down and made it to a chair by the table when there was a heavy thud against the cabin door. Devon staggered to the door and threw it fully open. He took a step or two onto the porch and looked about to see who had made the noise on his door. As he went to take another step, he felt something under the toe of his boot. Instinctively, he looked down. Just then, a cloud cleared the moon and, in the full light from it, there, under his foot on the porch, he saw a Narragansett war club he instantly recognized.

Devon drew his foot back and recoiled from the object. He looked in all directions looking for the source of this object. He felt his head begin to throb. He realized he was dizzy from drinking. He leaned down awkwardly and picked up the war club. He held it in front of him slightly dazed and, in the light coming through the open door of the cabin, he examined it. It was the one he had used to bludgeon his victim. There was still the stain of blood on the hard round stone.

Devon half-staggered to the end of the porch and threw it with all the strength he could muster as far into the back fields as he could. With staggering steps, Devon wobbled through the door of the cabin and slammed it behind him. He could not think clearly. He poured another cup of whiskey, then decided not to down it. He stood and went to the bucket of water beside the fireplace. Putting both hands into the bucket, Devon brought water to splash against his face. Just then, another thud came against the door!

Devon froze in place. He raced to the door and threw it open to see …NO! The war club lying on the porch exactly where it had just been. Devon was unable to approach it. He recoiled from it and stood muttering to himself that this was not possible. Then he heard the whistling again. Now from a new direction! Then from another direction. Devon backed slowly into the cabin, shut the door, and latched it. He stood with his back against the door trying to think through the events that were happening. Once he calmed himself, he realized the whistling had stopped. He turned and slowly opened the door.

He looked at the floor of the porch. There was nothing there. Devon stepped onto the porch and looked about. The moon was high, and clouds were scudding by on a light breeze. The light from the moon was bright enough to see objects when no clouds were near, but darker when the moon was obscured by clouds. As Devon looked about from the porch, he could see the crops poking through the earth in the south field, he could make out the tree line beyond. He could make out the break in the trees where the Pequot Trail continued south.

As he looked at the trail bathed in the light of the moon, he thought he saw something… someone, standing on the trail just at the trees. He could not make out more than just a silhouette, but, that silhouette: the hat, the cloak. No, it could not be! Could it? Devon turned and raced inside the cabin. His musket was propped against the wall just inside the door. He seized it in one hand and flew back out the door onto the porch. He levelled it in the direction of the figure he had seen ready to fire. There was nothing there. What trick were his eyes playing on him? Devon eased the cocked hammer of his fowling piece down and slowly retreated into the cabin.

Then it started again. The whistling! That God-awful melody! Devon went to the far corner of the cabin and sat on the floor drawing his legs up to his chest, his musket on the floor beside him. He covered his ears with his hands to shut out the noise.

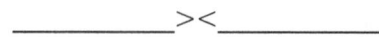

Wôquhsak arrived at the agreed meeting place at the far edge of the south field to find Mushqeenupeeash already there trying to catch his breath. On the ground in front of him lay one of the pahqumuhq[173]. Wôquhsak smiled and placed a second war club next to the one on the ground.

"I found the one he threw into the field," Mushqeenupeeash whispered smiling.

Nuhshwanum Nâhneepawuhshat appeared from the trees behind them and knelt between the boys.

"I believe your plan has worked," he said to Wôquhsak. "I think it is time for us to leave and return with tomorrow's moon." Wôquhsak nodded in agreement.

The group of three melted deeper into the trees without a sound until several rows of trees lay between them and the open field. When they were well away from the cabin, they could not help quietly celebrating the success of Wôquhsak's plan. As they crossed the Pequot Trail, they retrieved the cloak, hat, and internal structure of "Jules".

"Did you see how Devon reacted to the whistling?" Mushqeenupeeash said excitedly. "And throwing the pahqumuhq[174] against the cabin door …." Mushqeenupeeash could barely contain himself. "But, throwing the second one and then retrieving it …. That was brilliant!"

"I thought my lungs would explode I ran so fast to pick it up off the porch," Wôquhsak said. "I was so scared I thought my heart would leap from my chest." The three of them chuckled at this remark.

"I think the appearance and disappearance of the figure wearing Jules' cloak and hat really unnerved the man." Nuhshwanum

---

[173] Narragansett war club. Literally, 'head splitter'
[174] Ibid Footnote 171

Nâhneepawuhshat chimed in. "You have done well, my son. I am anxious to see what you have planned for tomorrow."

"I will tell you tonight, but, be assured, it will be more intense," Wôquhsak replied with a knowing smile.

FOURTEEN

WÔQUHSAK, MUSHQEENUPEEASH, AND NUHSHWANUM
Nâhneepawuhshat arrived back at their camp to find the fire had gone out. Nuhshwanum Nâhneepawuhshat directed Mushqeenupeeash to peel some pieces of bark from a nearby paper birch tree and, taking them from him, Nuhshwanum Nâhneepawuhshat slid the thin bark beneath the few remaining embers and gently blew on them until a flame rekindled. He then piled some dry pine needles on the small flame and then added some small twigs and ever larger twigs until a good fire was established. It was then they realized how late it was and how hungry they were. The moon was beginning to set. More than food, they all wanted sleep. Their hunger would wake them soon enough.

The morning dawned with a thick fog lying close to the ground. It wet every surface and penetrated the wood for their fire. But the three Narragansetts shook off the cool morning air, rekindled their fire, and gathered around the growing warmth of their hearth. Wôquhsak looked up at the bright spot in the fog where the sun was rising and wondered if there would be fog this night. As he thought about how that might play in his plan, Mushqeenupeeash arrived back at the camp having checked his snares. Breakfast would be two large rabbits.

"Do you think we should see what Devil Devon is doing this morning?" Wôquhsak's father asked almost sarcastically. "I would guess he has a big head this morning after all the strong water we saw him drinking."

"I think it helped our plan last night," Mushqeenupeeash said as he skinned the hides from the rabbits for breakfast.

"We can only hope he remembers what happened last night and is beginning to question what he thinks he heard and saw," Wôquhsak added. "We should watch his movements today and prepare for to-night."

Devon awoke still huddled in the corner of the cabin. His musket still lay on the floor beside him. His head was pounding from the whis-key he had consumed the day and night before. His mouth felt like dust and tasted worse. He roused himself and stood with a little diffi-culty. Attempting to step over his firearm he kicked it with the toe of his boot instead. He went to the bucket of water near the fireplace thinking to wash his face and to have a drink. It was nearly empty. He took hold of the rope handle and, feeling the weight of the wooden bucket more than normally in his weakened state, headed out to the well behind the cabin.

The fog that shrouded the cabin when Devon opened the door gave an eerie feeling to the scene. He could see no more than five or six feet around him the fog was so thick. Shifting the bucket to his left hand, Devon went to the end of the porch and stepped off in the di-rection of the well situated about ten feet from the rear of the cabin. The ground and plants along the path leading to the well left his boots wet from the dew.

He lowered the bucket attached to the well rope into the well until he heard it splash in the water below. As he let it sit for a few moments so it would fill, he set the bucket he held in his hand on the ground beside the well. He looked about through the dense fog. He was re-membering what he could about what had occurred the night before. Had it all really happened? Or was it the whiskey and he had dreamt the whole thing lying on the floor of the cabin. It was still and quiet standing in the fog this morning.

Still unsure of his experiences of the night before, he hauled the well bucket up to the top of the well and poured its contents into the bucket he had taken from the cabin. Devon dropped the well bucket again and retrieved it filled with water. He set the well bucket on the top of the stones forming the wall of the well and tossed water onto his face, then drank from his cupped hands. The water was cool and refreshing. He was beginning to feel a little better.

While he stood for a moment letting that better feeling sink in, He realized he was near the place where the war club he had thrown the night before, if he had thrown it, should have landed. To prove to himself that what had happened last evening was real, he would need to find that war club. Then he would know he had not imagined the sounds and sights he knew could not have happened.

He walked into the back field and searched for the war club. He covered the entire open area all the way to the tree line and even into the trees, though he doubted he had thrown the club that far. He found nothing. Did this mean his mind had played a trick on him? But he remembered picking up the weapon, feeling it in his grasp, and throw-ing it. It had happened. He knew it had happened. And if that had happened, had everything else happened? Was it real?

Devon returned to the well and picked up the bucket of water. He began the short walk to the front of the cabin still questioning if the events of the preceding night had been real or imagined. Just then, the sound of whistling broke through his thoughts. The fog was so thick he could not tell from what direction it emanated, but the melody he knew well. He broke into a trot and hopped onto the porch spilling some of the water from the bucket. He entered the cabin and closed the door securing it.

—————————>< —————————

Mushqeenupeeash had been watching the cabin when Devon appeared with a water bucket in his hand. He watched as Devon went to the well and dropped the bucket in to fill it with water. Mushqeenupeeash then watched the strange behavior of Devon as he walked through the back fields obviously looking for something. Then he realized what Devon was doing: he was looking for the pahqumuhq[175] he had thrown the night before. Mushqeenupeeash softly chuckled to himself knowing the club had already been retrieved.

As Mushqeenupeeash continued to watch Devon go back to the well and begin returning to the cabin, a thought struck Mushqeenupeeash. He began to softly whistle Jules' tune. He watched the effect it had on Devon and knew he needed to share it with the others back at camp.

Wôquhsak was seated, leaning against one of the boulders that helped hide their camp, when Mushqeenupeeash came into camp. He was looking at his father who stood not far from the hat and cloak of Jules still arrayed on the structure they had constructed of branches lashed with vines.

"I have something to tell you, Wôquhsak," Mushqeenupeeash said with excitement. "What we did last night has begun to have an effect, I think."

Wôquhsak and his father turned to hear what Mushqeenupeeash had to say. After hearing Devon's reaction to the soft whistling of Jules' melody, Wôquhsak and Nuhshwanum Nâhneepawuhshat began thinking how they could increase the pressure on Devon when night fell.

Wôquhsak returned to his seat leaning against one of the boulders. He was looking at his father who was still standing not far from the

---

[175] Narragansett war club. Literally 'head splitter'

hat and cloak. He was noticing how tall his Father was. Of the three of them, he was the tallest. At that moment, an idea came to Wôquhsak. He turned to Mushqeenupeeash who was standing near to him.

"Look," he said softly tapping Mushqeenupeeash's leg, "do you see how tall my father is?"

Mushqeenupeeash looked at Nuhshwanum Nâhneepawuhshat and nodded, agreeing with a statement that was obviously true.

"Do you think he would be willing to wear Jules' clothes?" Wôquhsak whispered.

"What are you two talking about," Nuhshwanum Nâhneepawuhshat suddenly spoke. "I see you looking at me in a way I am not comfortable with," he continued.

"I was noticing, Father, you are almost as tall as neetôpâwun[176] Jules," Wôquhsak began. "Not just as tall but you might be mistaken for him from a distance."

"What are you thinking, my son?" Nuhshwanum Nâhneepawuhshat questioned.

"If it was necessary to accomplish our goal," Wôquhsak continued a bit hesitantly, "would you agree to impersonating neetôpâwun Jules?"

"You are asking a great deal of me, Wôquhsak," Nuhshwanum Nâhneepawuhshat replied. "I must think on this and ask the spirit of Jules to allow it."

"I ask, Father, only as a last resort. If we can see Devon is close to breaking," Wôquhsak replied quickly following his request.

Nuhshwanum Nâhneepawuhshat turned from the camp and walked beyond the boulder he had been standing by. He needed time to think over the idea of wearing the garments of his murdered friend. For now, conversation on the subject ended.

Wôquhsak knew what he was asking of his father went against much of their beliefs in the sanctity of life and respect for the dead. It

---

[176] Friend

had never been part of his original plan. The idea had just occurred to him as he watched his father standing near the hat and cloak wrapped over the tree branches. He dismissed further thought of it and was somewhat upset for even thinking of it, let alone suggesting it. Other than height, his father bore no likeness of Jules. Such a ruse could only work if Nuhshwanum Nâhneepawuhshat's face was not visible or obscured in some way. For now, Wôquhsak would make plans for the coming night without considering this proposal. There was the entire day left to plan what could be done to drive Devon to question his belief in the supernatural.

FIFTEEN

IN THE EARLY AFTERNOON, NUHSHWANUM NÂHNEEPAW-
uhshat decided to return to the clan's summer encampment to see what
was happening there. He could hunt a bit on the way there in case he
needed to explain his absence from camp the past few days. He would
return before sunset to the temporary camp of his son and nephew.
He might even have some of Upeeshâwônkoon's cooking with him
when he returned. She would want to be sure her sons were eating well.

While his father was gone, Wôquhsak and Mushqeenupeeash began staging the plans for the evening. From what Mushqeenupeeash
had seen with Devon's reaction in the morning to merely hearing whistling, Wôquhsak wanted to continue to use that. He had questioned
Devon's reactions the prior night because of the drink he had consumed. But his reaction this morning was without any drink and, more
likely, nursing a hangover. There was no way of knowing if Devon
would drink again this night. Just as there was no way to know if there
would be clouds around the moon or fog to help hide a whistling
shadow.

As the sun began to move toward sunset, Nuhshwanum
Nâhneepawuhshat returned to the encampment bearing food from
Wôquhsak's mother. The dried fish and corn bread with honey were

gratefully received, but the news his father brought was not. When the Elders learned of his return to the encampment, they asked to see him.

"The Kuhchâyak[177] told me they had been visited by the wôpusuwak[178] this morning," Nuhshwanum Nâhneepawuhshat related. "They had been warned of their coming. The white men were cordial, but stern. Neechay Williams[179] was with them and spoke for them. There was no violence – this time."

"Did they search any of our houses?" Wôquhsak asked, concerned that the iron cooking pot might have been found.

"The Kuhchâyak[180] told me no," Nuhshwanum Nâhneepawuhshat replied, "but I dug a pit in the soft earth and wrapped your gift in skins before I buried it. Your mother only had it in a basket behind the house."

"That was our fault, Father," Wôquhsak said. "We left so quickly we had no time to hide it well."

"The Elders wanted to know how much longer you will need to accomplish your plan?" Nuhshwanum Nâhneepawuhshat continued, "The wôpusuwak[181] said they would return if the ones who killed Jules are not brought forward. I told the Elders your plan had started, and it appeared to be working."

"I would hope to turn Devon to the truth well before the moon is full," Wôquhsak said hoping for the best. "We will have a better idea after tonight."

"But, Father," Wôquhsak said a bit puzzled, "you said the Elders knew the wôpusuwak were coming. How is this possible?"

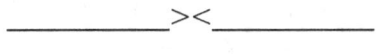

---

177 Elders
178 White Men
179 Brother Williams. Roger Williams
180 Ibid Footnote 177
181 Ibid Footnote 178

Devon stood with his back against the inside of the door of the cabin. He could faintly hear the last few notes of someone or something whistling beyond the door. He stood, still holding the water bucket, absent-mindedly. He knew what he had seen and heard last night was not possible. He could blame those phantoms from last night on the hard liquor he had consumed. But now, now was the day, and he had just experienced the phantom sounds of a tune whistled by a dead man. He would need a drink to calm his shaken nerves.

One dram led to another, and another, until the first cask was drained of its contents. Devon grew braver with each tipple, more assured that what he had heard was an impossibility. His mind was playing tricks on him. Even the figure he had seen on the Pequot Trail at the distance could be explained as only a shadow. After all, the dead do not rise again.

As the sun began to set, Devon was well into his second cask of whiskey. Should he finish this one, he could obtain more from the trading post tomorrow. After all, he still had some of the money he had stolen from the cabin. The whiskey had emboldened his confidence in his ability to deal with any situation, including any apparition that came his way.

Devon retrieved his musket from where it had laid on the floor the entire day. He placed it on the table in front of him. He did not think he had fired it the night before and he used the ramrod to check if it was loaded. It was. He would take care of any roving man or ghost that came to his door. He poured himself another cup of courage and watched the sun set.

He awoke with a start in near total darkness. The light of the moon streamed through the window set in the south wall of the cabin. Devon was not sure how long he had been asleep, nor was he sure what had awakened him. He used his hand to wipe his eyes and face. The bucket of water was still by the cabin door. Devon rose from his chair and drunkenly stumbled to the bucket. He knelt and threw water on his face with both hands. He was bent over the water bucket, water dripping from his features when he heard it. He rolled over and sat with his back against the door and listened for a few moments. The whistling was faint but shrill. The melody, all too familiar. He closed his eyes.

THUD! Thud. The door vibrated with the force of the blows made from the outside. THUD! THUD! It seemed that the door would splinter under the force of the blows. Devon could see his musket on the table across the room, but he was afraid if he took his weight from against the door, it might be forced open. Finally, he decided to take the chance and scrambled across the floor to reach the barrel of his musket. He pulled back the hammer and aimed at the middle of the door; his finger trembled near the trigger.

"Come on!" Devon screamed, "Show yerself, whatever ya' are! I've got a load of shot waitin' fer ya' here! Show yerself, I say!"

It was then Devon realized the whistling had ceased. The only sounds were the night creepers. He lowered his musket to his waist and advanced to the cabin door. Musket at the ready, Devon slowly cracked the door open. The sounds of the night peepers increased in volume. The moon was made milky by the fog bank that had rolled in after sunset. Forms were distorted by the shifting fog, as it seemed to move in waves of thickness. They would appear and disappear as the density of the fog changed. Devon scanned the floor of the porch expecting to see a war club that he suspected had been used to pound on the cabin door. In the moonlight he saw nothing. He moved further onto the porch raising his musket to a ready position.

As he scanned the fog-shrouded fields to the south of the cabin, the moonlight was more defused than normal and made the haze of light distort the growing plants into indistinguishable forms. Devon watched the clouds of fog sweep by his view feeling some calm for the first time in days. As he watched, a clear path between the clouds of fog allowed him to see further down the Pequot Trail to where it split the tree line.

Suddenly, he thought he saw movement. Yes, there it was. A form barely visible in the shade cast by the trees in the moonlight. He raised his fowling piece and tried to aim it; his eyes blurred from drink. He slowly began squeezing the trigger, bracing for the impact from the explosion against his shoulder when the rifle fired. He heard the click releasing the hammer and tensed for the recoil and heard the fizzle of a misfire.

Standing in the misting fog, the small amount of powder in the pan had become damp enough not to fire. He looked at the spot where he had thought a form was and saw nothing; he heard only the sounds of the night. As he turned to go back inside the cabin, the fog before the cabin thinned out for an instant. There before him, next to the large elm at the far end of the path leading to the Pequot Trail, he thought he distinguished a figure. For just a few seconds it was visible, Devon saw the hat, its tilted brim, the high crown; it was him! It was Jules! Just as the figure was disappearing in denser fog, Devon levelled his musket and pulled the trigger. Nothing happened. In his fear, he had forgotten the misfire! Devon looked up as the fog thinned out again. The figure was gone.

Slowly, Devon withdrew into the cabin. He sat in the chair at the table in darkness, too shaken to light a lantern, let alone a candle. He dropped the musket on the table. Devon saw the whiskey cask on the table. He did not want any drink. He wanted to understand what had just happened. Devon softly swore under his breath. It had only been a matter of fifteen yards away! It was an easy shot. He looked at the flintlock on the table. The powder in the pan was too little and too wet to ignite. But he was sure he had seen it! But what was it? Who was it? If it was the same shadowy form he thought he saw in the shade of the tree, how did it move so swiftly?

Then it started again. The whistling started again. He tried to cover his ears with the palms of his hands. The whistling grew louder. It seemed to come from every direction. Devon was about to cry out when the door of the cabin suddenly flew open. Just off the path leading to the porch stood a figure dressed in a dark cloak and the hat of Jules, its face in shadow. It slowly raised its right arm and pointed at Devon. At that moment, the fog fell away, and Devon clearly saw it was the image of his victim. It was Jules de Vendome. He was sure of it!

Devon was shaking violently as he let out a blood-chilling scream of terror and lunged forward to slam the cabin door. He kept his weight against the door, fearing not to would allow the specter's entry. Knowing his musket was useless, his eyes searched the cabin for another weapon. There, on the north wall hung Jules' sword. It was thin and appeared light but, at least, it was a weapon. Devon decided in an instant to grab the weapon. He rolled from the door and sprung to his feet, reaching for the handle of the sword at the same moment. Pulling it from the mounting on the wall, Devon now felt he could defend himself. He crossed the room in only a few steps and, holding the weapon's slim blade before him, pulled open the door to see…. nothing! He wheeled to his left, then his right. And there was nothing. He cautiously stepped off the porch to where the figure had stood. He looked at the ground looking for footprints. All he saw was the compacted earth of the path.

Devon slowly backed toward the cabin porch. The fog was thinning and the light from the moon was growing. Devon held the saber in front of him as he surveyed the area around him. He heard no whistling, no sounds other than the night peepers. He felt the step onto the porch with the back of his boot and mounted the steps onto the porch without turning around. Slowly, he backed into the cabin and closed the door. He knew what he had seen! But how were there no boot prints? Devon would not sleep the rest of this night.

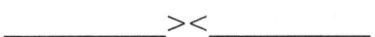

Wôquhsak and Mushqeenupeeash reached their spot at the edge of the south field nearly at the same moment. Both were out of breath and excited by what had taken place.

"That was very brave of you," Mushqeenupeeash complimented Wôquhsak in a hushed voice.

"What are you talking about?" Wôquhsak replied.

"Putting on the cloak and hat of Jules and standing in front of the porch," Mushqeenupeeash whispered, a bit surprised at Wôquhsak's reply.

"That was not me," Wôquhsak said. "I thought it was you! And I wondered how you managed to do it so quickly!"

At that moment, a deep, wispy voice from behind them said softly, "It was me."

The two young boys turned to see a figure still dressed in the cloak and hat standing just inside the tree line. A tremor of fear ran through the two of them raising the hair on their arms. It was Nuhshwanum Nâhneepawuhshat.

"You scared us out of our skins," Wôquhsak blurted out before he could stop it.

Nuhshwanum Nâhneepawuhshat squatted down and laughed softly.

"I think it may have had a similar effect on our Devon," he said as he nodded toward the cabin where no light could be seen.

"But if it was you before the cabin," Mushqeenupeeash began with a question in his voice, "how did he not find prints from your ma-husunash[182]? Even moccasins leave a footprint."

"Not if you stand on a pelt," Nuhshwanum Nâhneepawuhshat said with a smile. "It is not good for the fur, but it leaves no footprint."

"But you took a risk knowing he has a firestick," Wôquhsak replied with concern.

---

[182] Moccasins

"I saw the spark and puff of smoke from when it did not fire. It had not fired earlier, and I did not think he had tried to find out why," Nuhshwanum Nâhneepawuhshat replied. "But do not tell your mother what I did."

The three them giggled at Nuhshwanum Nahneepawuhshat's joking admonishment and slid into the forest to head back to their camp. The three of them would rest well the remainder of the night. Wôquhsak was sure Devon was close to confessing.

SIXTEEN

THE REST OF THE NIGHT PASSED WITHOUT INCIDENT. morning dawned clear and sunny. Wôquhsak was up early thinking of what could be done this coming night to push Devon over the edge to insanity. The news Wôquhsak's father had brought from the clan's leaders told Wôquhsak that time was running out to have his plan succeed in making Devon believe he was going to be haunted forever by his victim. Wôquhsak had an idea, but it would take some work and a great deal of luck. He needed to talk with the others about his thoughts.

As the three braves - for Wôquhsak and Mushqeenupeeash had certainly proven themselves - sat around the morning fire, Wôquhsak began sharing his idea for what he hoped would be something that would push Devon into admitting what he had done to his white brethren.

"Father," he began, "do you think we could make something that might resemble the hat and cloak of Jules?" His companions looked at him with no understanding of his question.

"What I mean is, could we make something that, if seen at a distance, could be mistaken for Jules dressed in his cloak and hat?"

"I know what you are asking, Wôquhsak," his father said. "Even if it were possible, neither of you are tall enough to pass for our friend Jules."

"But together we could be more than tall enough to pass," Wôquhsak replied.

"What are you thinking?" Nuhshwanum Nâhneepawuhshat said to his son.

"If we could confront Devon with something that would seem completely impossible ...," Wôquhsak's voice trailed off.

"What are you thinking, my son?" his father coaxed him to continue.

"It is just a thought, and it is not completely formed," Wôquhsak mused. "Let me think on it a bit longer."

"If this idea involves what you asked before about fashioning a hat and cloak like neetôpâwun[183] Jules' we have nothing here with which to do that. We would need the help of the women of our clan, and they would need time."

"But could it be possible?" Wôquhsak asked.

"The women of our clan are very good with the needle and sewing," Nuhshwanum Nâhneepawuhshat replied, "and most of them knew Jules and would know his clothes. If it did not need to be more than just similar, it could be done quicker."

"Would you, Father, return to our clan's camp and ask for help?" Wôquhsak meekly asked. "After all, the Elders said they would help in any way we asked them."

Nuhshwanum Nâhneepawuhshat nodded in agreement.

"I will take the hat with me," he said. "It is the most distinctive part and most recognizable from a distance. The cloak could easily be mimicked by a blanket or hide."

Having agreed to attempt to enlist the clan's help in Wôquhsak's plan, Nuhshwanum Nâhneepawuhshat rose from the fire and respectfully lifted Jules' hat from where he had placed it the previous night and carefully folded it so it would fit into his hunting pouch. He slipped the long strap over his head and moved the bag, so it lay against his

---

[183] Our friend

back. He would be able to move more swiftly through the woods with the bag on his back and the contents would be better protected.

"Father," Wôquhsak said, "please tell them time is important, and thank them for helping."

"I will tell them," his father replied as he started to leave the camp. "And I will return before dark to help tonight."

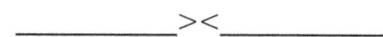

Devon had slept fitfully. Every time he closed his eyes, he saw the figure of Jules standing in front of him and relived raising his musket and hearing only the hollow "click" of the musket's hammer hitting a flash pan, empty of powder. He would wake with a start at the sound of the misfire and curse himself for not filling that pan with gunpowder.

Upon waking, Devon realized the grumbling in his stomach was from hunger. He had not really eaten anything the day before. He began foraging through the shelves and larder of the cabin. The bread he found was stale and hard. A small cheese was overripe, but still edible. A small jug of cider would taste better than the whiskey that was still in the second cask.

As Devon sat down to attempt to eat his meager repast, he glanced out the window at the field beyond. How foolish he was to be eating this rotting food when an entire garden of vegetables lay just beyond the window! He rose from the table and began to walk to the door when he suddenly realized what could be waiting for him outside. He turned and grabbed the hilt of the saber that was lying on the floor. He would not be unarmed.

Opening the cabin door, he cautiously came out onto the porch. The rumbling of hunger in his stomach urged him toward the garden. He quickly pulled a small head of lettuce from the ground and proceeded to savage the rows of young carrot, radish, and spring onion. The pea plants were small with pods only partly developed but Devon stripped a few of the pods anyway. With his fear mounting, Devon clutched his treasures tightly in the crook of his arm and quickly returned to the cabin. He would have plenty to eat on this day.

Wôquhsak and Mushqeenupeeash sat in their camp planning their strategy for the coming night. They wanted to keep the pressure building on Devon. Wôquhsak did not know what his father would be told by the Elders about further help he was asking from the clan. He did not know how quickly the task he was asking his clan to perform could be completed, or if it could be completed at all. He knew the wôpusu-wak[184] had already come to his clan's summer camp, and he could easily assume they had visited many other summer camps of other clans. How much longer would the white men be willing to wait peaceably for one of the people to admit guilt? Time was growing short and Wôquhsak could not be sure his plan would work quickly enough to save the lives of his people. What was it going to take to unhinge Devon?

Wôquhsak and Mushqeenupeeash realized they had used every tactic they could think of employing, and it had not been enough. While the whistling had been effective and the war club appearing and disappearing as well, nothing had been as effective as the ghostly appearance of Jules. Was there something more they could do they had not thought of? Even the weather had provided everything from full moonlight and clouds one night followed by dense fog the next. Wôquhsak had a germ of an idea whirling in his mind, but it refused to completely come together.

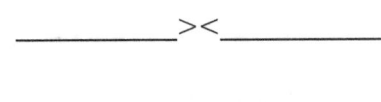

[184] White Men

After eating his fill of the early spring bounty from the garden, Devon sat back enjoying the small jug of cider he had found in the larder. It had started to harden and had a slight spice to it he was enjoying. The realization that another night was coming, along with whatever terrors it might hold, motivated Devon to take action. He would not be caught unprepared this night.

Devon checked his powder horn and realized it was less than half full. He looked around the cabin, searching for powder he knew had to be somewhere. Jules had to have a cache of gunpowder somewhere. It was only reasonable to think a supply of powder would be kept living on the edge of a wilderness with hostiles around you. On the floor of the larder, Devon found a small barrel of powder. He filled his powder horn and proceeded to charge the flash pan of his musket and his pistol. He checked to be sure they were both loaded once again. He set the musket at the ready by the door of the cabin. He left the pistol on the table near the larder.

He was feeling more confident about the coming of darkness because now he was ready. He sat at the table and picked up the saber that lay on it. It was a pretty weapon, its curved blade was light, yet strong. The guard in front of the hilt was intricately woven of metal. The balance of the weapon made it easy to wield. He noticed the blade held an inscription in a language he did not know. "Veritas mea Est" (Truth is Mine) he read in a beautiful script. Perhaps it was better he did not know the meaning.

As the sun passed midday and began to set in the west, Devon had recovered his sense of confidence and swagger. He took a short tin cup from the cupboard and poured a small quantity of whiskey from the second cask.

It was getting late in the day. Wôquhsak's father had not returned to their camp. Wôquhsak was becoming concerned. Had something happened when he arrived at the clan's summer camp? Had the wôpusuwak[185] returned to the encampment? Had his father stumbled into their presence at the camp? Had the wôpusuwak discovered Jules' hat when they searched his bag? Wôquhsak kept these thoughts to himself, so they did not upset Mushqeenupeeash. If his father did not return by the time the moon rose, it would be left to just two of them to conduct the plans for the night. And those plans would need to be changed if they were to be performed only by the two of them.

The two boys ate a meager meal of berries and roasted squirrel. At least there was plenty of squirrel to go around as Mushqeenupeeash had trapped four. Since Nuhshwanum Nâhneepawuhshat had taken Jules' hat with him, there could be no appearance of an apparition this night. This would weaken their ability to haunt Devon. It would not be worth having a ghostly form appear if Nuhshwanum Nâhneepawuhshat was unsuccessful in getting a similar hat fashioned by the clan.

The sun had set, and the moon was rising in a cloudless sky. Its light would be strong on the landscape tonight. Wôquhsak was about to tell Mushqeenupeeash that the plans they had made for tonight would need to change when Nuhshwanum Nâhneepawuhshat appeared with a smile on his face. Over his arm, along with Jules' hat, was a leather creation that had somewhat the same shape as the hat. On top of that lay a leather hood with eye holes. Above a thin slit of a mouth was a hole cut for a nose.

---

[185] White Men

SEVENTEEN

THE HOOTING OF AN OWL SOMEWHERE IN THE TREES near the cabin put Devon on alert. He was already on edge. The moon had been up for quite some time and there had been nothing other than the sounds of the night. Devon had listened intently for something, anything, that would indicate whatever, or whoever, was about. Then he heard it.

The whistled melody floated on the light night breeze. The direction was unclear. Or was it coming from more than one direction? Was it echoing among the trees? Devon could not be sure. He knew what he had experienced the past two nights was about to begin again. But this time, he was prepared. His musket was loaded, checked and ready.

Devon decided he was going to take the initiative and meet head-on whatever or whoever was at the cabin this night. He blew out the one candle he had allowed to give him light and advanced to the cabin door. He listened intently. Yes, it was the tune Jules always whistled. It was the tune he was whistling when Devon had accosted him on the Pequot Trail the day he killed him. He tried to open the cabin door as slowly as possible to see if he could determine from what direction the whistling emanated. He stayed close to the wall of the cabin under the shadow of the roof of the porch and looked about in the bright moonlight. He held his musket tightly against his chest. The whistling seemed to come from his right. somewhere beyond the planted field. Then it came from his left somewhere distant beyond in the trees. And then it stopped.

It felt like an eternity to Devon as he stood in the shadow waiting for something – what, he did not know. He closed his eyes and listened intently. Nothing but the night creepers could be heard. He opened his eyes, his nerves beginning to fray. Devon looked to his right. Where the Pequot Trail made a slight bend to the east at the far end of the south field, where the tree line began, Devon sensed something. A figure standing in the shadow cast by the trees in the moonlight. He peered at the figure to be sure. Unlike the previous night, the figure was there: absolutely! As the shadow started to shrink back toward the trees as the moon continued its arc across the sky, he finally saw what he was looking for: the hat!

Devon shouldered his musket and pulled back the hammer. It would be a long-range shot, but he thought he could reach it. He checked for wind, closed his left eye, centered his target, and squeezed the trigger. The bright flash of light from the end of the barrel blinded Devon for a second as the powder ignited. The sound of the explosion silenced the night. As Devon's night vision returned, he saw the specter begin to slump and fall. He smiled broadly and breasted his musket.

At that instant, a loud THUD shook the boards of the porch on which he stood. Devon turned to his left in time to see a war club skittering toward him on the porch. Looking to the end of the porch his eyes beheld the impossible. Standing on the edge of the porch was a figure dressed in the hat and cloak of Jules de Vendome. It had no face, only eyes!

Devon stumbled backward, his mouth agape, his hands trembling as they opened reflexively and dropped the useless musket. As he backed away from this specter, he fell on his back on the rough boards of the porch unable to release the scream his throat held. As he pushed away from this ghost of his victim on his elbows and heels, the thing reached down and picked up the war club. Club in hand, the figure began advancing toward him.

In desperation, Devon finally was able to let out an inhuman scream as he rolled off the porch and ran from the cabin. Reaching the Pequot Trail, he turned in the direction of the trading posts. As he disappeared, his wild screams faded into the night air as he ran.

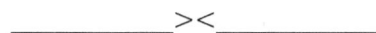

Nuhshwanum Nâhneepawuhshat watched as the terrified man fled from the porch. His greater concern at this moment was his son beyond the south field. The plan had been for Wôquhsak to stand on Mushqeenupeeash to simulate the height of Jules. The hat fashioned by the clan that day would never have passed for Jules' stylish apparel up close, but from a distance, it was a fair match. They had attempted to measure the distance from the cabin so a musket shot would either fall short or cause little damage if it struck. But Nuhshwanum Nâhneepawuhshat had seen the figure wrapped in a blanket fall to the ground. Even though he wanted to know where Devon was running to, he needed to know his son was unharmed.

He shed the cloak and the hat and tore the leather mask from his head dropping it onto the porch and sprinted out to the Pequot Trail and turned south, running now as fast as he could. As he got closer to the spot where Wôquhsak and Mushqeenupeeash had made their appearance, he saw nothing in the moonlight on the pathway.

A voice from the trees softly called his name. It was Wôquhsak. Lying beside him under the tree shaded from the moon's light, was Mushqeenupeeash. Blood dripped from a wound in his thigh. Wôquhsak was holding a clump of moss in a piece of deerskin against the wound.

"How did this happen?" Nuhshwanum Nâhneepawuhshat asked a bit confused.

"It is my fault," Wôquhsak replied. "At the last minute, Mushqeen-upeeash decided it would be better for him to stand on me, since I am older and stronger."

Nuhshwanum Nâhneepawuhshat removed the poultice Wôquh-sak had pressed against the wound and saw the wound was only a graze and had already stopped bleeding. It would be a prized scar of bravery but nothing fatal.

"We must hurry, Father," Wôquhsak said. "The rest of the plan must be carried out. We will leave Mushqeenupeeash here until we can return." Mushqeenupeeash nodded his agreement and encouraged his companions to go. He would be fine hidden as he was from the trail.

Wôquhsak and his father ran to the cabin and retrieved the pah-qumuhq[186], hat, mask, and cloak from the porch. They returned to the Pequot Trail and began following Devon's escape route. They had no thought of catching up to him for he was long gone. But they were not quite done with him yet this night.

---

[186] Narragansett war club. Literally, 'head splitter'

EIGHTEEN

WÔQUHSAK WAS HOPING DEVON WOULD SEEK SANCTU-
ary at the first place he would come upon among his own kind: the
trading posts. He and his father would complete the plan now that
Mushqeenupeeash lay in the protective shade of a tree beside the Pequot Trail. If Devon were as terrified as he seemed to be, the last part
of the plan would surely unhinge him completely.

Nuhshwanum Nâhneepawuhshat carried the cloak of Jules draped
over his arm and the war club, while Wôquhsak carried Jules' hat, and
the leather mask cradled in his arms. They hurried along the Pequot
trail northward toward the smaller path that led to the trading posts.
They knew the hour was still well before sunrise because the moon had
not set, though it was low in the sky. If Devon had reached the trading
posts, it was unlikely anyone would be awake so early, but his arrival
would certainly rouse anyone there. They would need to approach cautiously.

Reaching the trading post path, the father and son kept to the edge
of the path where the moonlight was blocked by the foliage. They approached in a low crouch listening intently. As they reached Brother
Williams' trading post, all was quiet.

"Neechay[187] Williams is not here," Nuhshwanum Nâhneepawuhshat whispered to Wôquhsak. "Loud voices are coming from Smith trading post. Move to where you can see the post but not be seen."

Nuhshwanum Nâhneepawuhshat handed Wôquhsak the pahqumuhq[188] and took the leather mask and hat, tapped his son reassuringly on the shoulder, and crossed the path, disappearing into the trees and bushes on the far side of the path. Wôquhsak moved a bit closer to the second trading post keeping low and following the edge of the cove. He reached a point where he could see the men talking on the porch and he was well hidden in marsh grass. A group of men were standing on the porch, their faces showing in the light of a fire burning on the grassy area in front of the porch. Beside the fire a figure on his knees was pleading with the men. Most had a look of disbelief on their faces at what the man kneeling was saying. One or two people began to snicker at his pleas. As the kneeling man turned slightly, Wôquhsak saw it was Devon. He was distraught and pleading with his audience. Although Wôquhsak did not understand the words, it was obvious Devon was now convinced.

As Wôquhsak watched, he saw a figure emerge at the far corner of the building just far enough to catch the firelight. It was Nuhshwanum Nâhneepawuhshat wearing the cloak, mask, and hat. At that moment, Devon turned back to the group of men on the porch to again plead his truth. Out of the corner of his eye, he saw what he believed was the ghost of his victim. He let forth a scream that sounded inhuman and rented the night air as he skittered away from the fire in fear. The men on the porch stood in shocked silence. Devon pointed in the direction of the specter, but it was now gone, and his audience saw nothing.

The confusion of the men and their attempts to calm Devon allowed Wôquhsak to slip back along the trail unnoticed to the shadows

---

[187] Brother
[188] Narragansett war club. Literally 'head splitter'

where his father had left him. Nuhshwanum Nâhneepawuhshat quietly burst from the far side of the path and motioned for Wôquhsak to follow him down the path toward the Pequot Trail. In a loping run they turned onto the trail and ran toward the place where Jules had been killed. Nuhshwanum Nâhneepawuhshat told Wôquhsak to replace the hat and cloak where he had originally found them in the crevice of the outcrop on the west side of the trail. He then had Wôquhsak place the pahqumuhq[189] where he had first found it when Jules was slain at the edge of the trail.

"Now we wait," Nuhshwanum Nâhneepawuhshat whispered and motioned to the top of the rock outcrop. Wôquhsak was a bit confused. This had not been part of his plan. In fact, since he and his father had started for the trading posts following Devon, nothing had been part of his plan. But he followed his father as they scrambled up to the flat rock where he and Mushqeenupeeash had witnessed Jules' murder. They lay flat on the rock near the edge where they could see the trail. Even though the day had been warm, the rock felt cool against their clothing as it was bathed in the setting moonlight. Nuhshwanum Nâhneepawuhshat cautioned his son to be still.

"What are we waiting for?" Wôquhsak whispered.

"I know little of the wôpusu's[190] language," Nuhshwanum Nâhneepawuhshat whispered back, "but I heard one of them tell Devon they wanted 'proof' of what he claimed."

"What proof, Father? There is none," Wôquhsak replied.

"Devon said he would show them someone had stolen Jules' hat and cloak to scare him," Nuhshwanum Nâhneepawuhshat whispered. "And just before I appeared, he had told them he would show them."

Wôquhsak now understood and lay quietly. It was not long before the glow of torches appeared on the trail.

---

[189] Narragansett war club
[190] White Man's

_____><_____

Devon led the group of men up the Pequot Trail confident that he could show them that someone was trying to play a trick on him. He knew the hat and cloak were no longer in the crevice under the ledge. He had looked for them when he fooled Barker into discovering the body of his victim. If nothing else, it would prove to Devon, himself, that what he had heard and seen were not figments of his own imagining, but the efforts of someone, he knew not who, to drive him mad. He did not believe in ghosts and phantoms.

The group of torch-lit men stopped just below the rock outcrop and Devon continued the tirade he had been delivering all the way from the trading post. He stood in the middle of the group claiming one or more of them were trying to drive him into admitting something. Someone was trying to implicate him in the murder of Jules de Vendome, and he was going to prove it. The group was expressing its skepticism with audible laughter and denials.

"I am telling you someone has been showing themselves at night in the moonlight dressed in that Frenchman's hat and cloak," Devon was saying. "And I can prove it!"

"Isn't this where Vendome was killed?" a member of the group standing slightly apart from the rest asked.

"Yeah, it is," another member nearer the group affirmed.

"It was down there in the bushes where we found him," another man in the group spoke up.

"Well, how did you miss this?" the man standing apart from the group said as he reached down just under a branch at the side of the trail and lifted a war club for all the others to see in the torch light. Devon recoiled at the sight of the pahqumuhq.[191]

"It even looks like it has blood on it," the man continued as he examined the rounded rock expertly attached to the shaft.

---

[191] Narragansett war club. Literally, 'head splitter'

"That wasn't there, I tell you!" Devon screamed as he fell to a sitting position, I tell you it wasn't there!"

"Hey, fellas," another member of the group standing near the rock ledge said, "look what I found," suddenly gaining everyone's attention,

The man held up the hat and cloak he had just found in the crevice in the outcrop. Devon's eyes widened when he saw the clothing.

"That can't be!" he screamed, "I put them there and they weren't there the last time I looked! I know they were gone. Someone had taken them. I... I..."

The boss of the group looked at Devon on the ground, his eyes wild with confusion, babbling nonsensical phrases, raising his hands to shield his eyes from the sight of Jules' hat and cloak.

"Devon?" the boss said menacingly, "what do you mean 'you put them there'?"

"I didn't say that" Devon replied stopping the irrational outburst he was directing at himself.

"We all heard it, Devon," the boss repeated sternly, taking the clothing from the man who had retrieved it from the crevice. He pushed them toward Devon, who screamed in terror and recoiled, moving to defend himself from the offering.

"What did you do, Devon?" the leader of the group said in loud demanding voice. "Tell us what you did, damn you!"

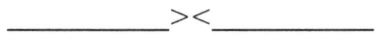

Wôquhsak and Nuhshwanum Nâhneepawuhshat peeped over the edge of the outcrop at the men below. Although they did not understand much of what was being said, their actions, and the reactions of Devon, spoke volumes. They watched Devon collapse to the ground and put his arms up defensively. They watched Devon's obvious denial of the war club. They watched his reaction to the presentation of Jules' clothing. They heard anger in the leader's voice.

They watched as Devon groveled on the ground mumbling unintelligible words. Occasionally, Nuhshwanum Nâhneepawuhshat thought he caught a word or two. But it did not matter; the meaning of what was unfolding before him and Wôquhsak was clear. Devon was no longer responding to the men about him. He was looking to them to protect him from something unseen. Wôquhsak and Nuhshwanum Nâhneepawuhshat watched as Devon got to his feet and began looking about with wild eyes.

One of the men in the group handed the leader a length of braided leather. He bound Devon's arms behind his back and the group started back up the trail toward the trading posts. Devon continued to look about wildly, mumbling to himself, as he stumbled along, no longer resisting in any way. The light from the torches and the conversation among the men faded as their distance from the ledge increased. Wôquhsak and Nuhshwanum Nâhneepawuhshat did not move until light from the torches was no longer visible on the trail.

Just as Wôquhsak and his father were about to climb down from the outcrop, Wôquhsak saw movement at the edge of the trail. He grabbed his father's arm to stop his father's movement. It was the whiskey lover from the trading post. He had followed the group of wôpusuwak[192] at a distance and stopped just off the trail watching. He did not move as the group of wôpusuwak[193] passed him unnoticed, crouching just off the trail. Once the group of men had passed him with the light of the torches casting shadows about them, the form came to its feet and followed the group keeping well back so as not to be discovered. He did not move as one who had imbibed too much fire water. In fact, he moved with great stealth. Wôquhsak was sure he had seen this person at the clan's summer camp and now he saw him again.

---

[192] White Men
[193] Ibid Footnote 192

NINETEEN

WÔQUHSAK AND HIS FATHER QUIETLY SLID DOWN THE side of the outcrop and trotted off down the Pequot Trail in the direction of Jules' cabin and the tree under which Mushqeenupeeash had been left. Wôquhsak thought about what he had seen as he trotted down the trail. He knew his plan had destroyed the psyche of its target. He hoped his people would be spared the misdirected wrath of the wôpusuwak[194], but he could find no mercy in his heart for the man Devon. Whatever punishment he would receive would not, and could not, replace the loss to the Narragansett of their friend Jules de Vendome. Friends like him and Brother Williams were few among the white men.

As the two passed Jules' cabin, Wôquhsak's thoughts returned to Mushqeenupeeash. They found him awake and uncomfortable, but anxious to know what had happened. Rather than take the time to tell him everything, Nuhshwanum Nâhneepawuhshat suggested they make their way to the clan's encampment while the light of the setting moon might still light their way. Telling Mushqeenupeeash what had happened could wait until they were back home. So, with that,

---

[194] White Men

Nuhshwanum Nâhneepawuhshat hoisted the injured boy over his shoulder and he and Wôquhsak headed for the bay and home.

Upeeshâwakoon had heard someone outside her lodge even before Nuhshwanum Nâhneepawuhshat and Wôquhsak stepped through the doorway carrying Mushqeenupeeash. She was surprised by the injury to the younger boy. She was happy to see her men but concerned for the wound Mushqeenupeeash had sustained. The sun was just rising across the great bay as she settled Mushqeenupeeash on his bed and began looking at his injury. She was relieved that it was not serious.

"Wôquhsak," she said sharply, "get me seawater and stop at the house of the pâwâw[195] and tell her we need her medicine. Take the tall pot with you. And, when you return, I want to know how this happened."

"The boy is tired, Mother," Wôquhsak heard his father speaking as he slipped out the doorway. It was true. They had been up the entire night, but his plan had appeared to work. Only time would tell if it had really been successful.

Wôquhsak returned with the high-necked ceramic container filled with cool salt water from the cove. He watched as his mother tenderly rinsed the wound. Mushqeenupeeash winced as the salt stung the open wound. Upeeshâwakoon had done this many times on many minor scrapes and cuts when Wôquhsak was younger. She expected the reaction and calmed the boy with a tenderness Wôquhsak remembered well.

A call from the doorway announced the pâwâw[196] carrying her bag of medicines. Upeeshâwakoon greeted the old woman warmly as she knelt next to her and began examining the wound from the musket ball. She chatted with Wôquhsak's mother as she worked cleaning the wound and taking some plants from her bag. Mixing them in a small

---

[195] Healer
[196] Ibid Footnote 195

bowl, she made a paste that she smeared into the wound. The clan had great respect for the medicinal knowledge of this healer. In a matter of a few minutes, she had finished her attendance of Mushqeenupeeash and was giving her final instructions to both Upeeshâwakoon and Mushqeenupeeash.

Upeeshâwakoon thanked the pâwâw and asked how she could reward her for her service. The medicine woman only suggested that she would appreciate a portion of Nuhshwanum Nahneepawuhshat's next hunt. This was accepted graciously by all present. Another round of thanks and she was through the door. Wôquhsak turned to say something to Mushqeenupeeash and found he was soundly asleep. It made him realize how tired he really was, and so, he too lay down and was soon asleep. Upeeshâwakoon looked at her two charges and decided she would let them sleep a few hours, but not the whole day. If they were home, she felt Wôquhsak's plan must have borne results. Besides, she could wait until they awoke to hear what had happened.

The three men had left without cleaning out their temporary camp, Nuhshwanum Nâhneepawuhshat told Upeeshâwakoon he needed to collect the things they had left in camp. She understood and only requested her husband to be quick so he would return by the time the boys awoke. Nuhshwanum Nâhneepawuhshat understood and left to gather any possessions they had left at their camp.

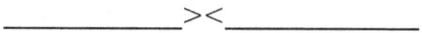

He stood at his full height at the entrance to the lodge of the Elders. He requested permission to enter as he furtively glanced around him. He wanted no one to take notice of him. Horned Owl entered the lodge and took a seat at the fire ring. He was greeted warmly by the Elders.

"What news do you bring us from the wôpusuwak[197]?" the oldest kuhchâyak[198] asked quietly.

"I cannot stay long, or I will be missed," Horned Owl said just above a whisper.

"We understand," the Elder continued, "we cannot put your place with the white men in jeopardy. The information you receive by your acceptance at the trading post is too important to risk its loss."

"How is it that they speak so freely around you?" another Elder questioned.

"They do not think I hear and understand them when they speak in their tongue," Horned Owl replied. "They only see me as a wretched form who is always drunk on their fire water whiskey. They do not know I pour it out."

"The one they call Devon has been taken by his fellow wôpusuwak[199]," Horned Owl announced to the kuhchâyak.[200] "They are holding him as he has admitted killing our friend, the Frenchman. He babbles to himself and laughs at nothing. They say he is mad."

The kuhchâyak[201] received this news with quiet nods of acknowledgement.

"What will be done with him?" one of the other Elders asked.

"They have sent to the big settlement across the bay for more wôpusuwak[202] to come and take him back with them," Horned Owl related. "This should happen in two suns."

"Where are they keeping this man Devon until he is taken across the pootupâq?"[203] the first Elder asked.

"He is locked in the storeroom in chains," said Horned Owl. "I can hear him ranting and laughing to himself from where I sit outside."

---

[197] White Men
[198] Elder
[199] Ibid Footnote 197
[200] Elders
[201] Ibid Footnote 198
[202] White Men
[203] The Narragansett Bay

"This news we will spread to the other clans," the oldest kuhchâyak[204] said. "It means our people are safe and will not be blamed for his act."

"There is one more thing I must tell you," Horned Owl spoke. "Your brave who saw the murder, he recognized me when I brought you warning of the wôpusuwak[205] coming. I think he must be told of my mission." The Elders nodded agreement.

The gentle shaking Wôquhsak felt of his shoulder woke him. It was his mother, Upeeshâwônkoon, letting him know he needed to awake. Mushqeenupeeash was still asleep beside his cousin and was not disturbed by Wôquhsak getting up. As Wôquhsak wiped the sleep from his eyes, he turned in the direction of the fire ring where his mother was sitting. He was still feeling his lack of sleep as he stood and stretched. His mother smiled at him.

"You father tells me your plan has worked," she said with pride in her voice.

"We think Devil Devon has said enough to the other wôpusuwak[206] that they know of his deed," Wôquhsak replied with an acknowledging nod.

At that moment, Nuhshwanum Nâhneepawuhshat stepped through the doorway holding the new cooking pot Wôquhsak had traded for at the trading post in what seemed a long time ago. The cast iron glistened as the last drops of water dripped off its bottom. Nuhshwanum Nâhneepawuhshat had used water to clean off the last bits of dirt clinging to it from the hole in which he had buried it. The wôpusuwak[207] would never have found it even if they had searched for

---

204 Elder
205 White Men
206 Ibid footnote 205
207 Ibid Footnote 205

it. Now that the killer of neetôpâwun Jules was known to all, there was no longer a need to conceal the new pot. But Wôquhsak's mother did not want to use the new pot yet. She motioned for her husband to place it against the back wall of the lodge. She would christen it with the first meal from the next deer hunt.

As the three of them sat about the fire talking quietly, Wôquhsak related to his mother what his plan had been and what had happened to Mushqeenupeeash. He took full responsibility for Mushqeenupeeash's injury. The conversation had stirred Mushqeenupeeash from his slumber. As he rolled over to see who was talking, he winced in pain. As Upeeshâwakoon came to his side to comfort him, a member of the clan appeared at the door of the lodge.

A quick conversation between Nuhshwanum Nâhneepawuhshat and the brave at the door ended with Wôquhsak's father motioning to his son to come to him.

"The Elders wish to see you," Nuhshwanum Nâhneepawuhshat told his son. "The brave did not know why. But they want to see you now."

Wôquhsak glanced at his mother who was listening intently and dashed out the door of the longhouse. Wôquhsak decided it would be better not to run through the camp to the Elder's lodge, and so he slowed to a deliberate, but rapid, walk. When he reached the lodge of the Elders, he announced himself and was bid to enter. As his eyes adjusted to the dimmer light of the hut, the Elders asked him to sit opposite them across the fire ring.

"Wôquhsak," the chief Elder began, "we are pleased to see you return to camp. This must mean your plan has succeeded."

"I believe it has," Wôquhsak began. "I saw the wôpusuwak[208] bind the arms of the killer and take him toward the trading posts."

"This is good to hear," the Elders all agreed, "but there is a matter we need to share with you that is of much importance."

---

[208] White Men

133

Wôquhsak tried not to betray his surprise at this statement from the Elders.

"There is someone here you must meet and never speak of," the second Elder spoke in a very somber tone. "Once you meet him, you must never admit to knowing him. In fact, you have already met him."

Wôquhsak then noticed another person standing in the shadows of the lodge. It was the brave he had seen at the trading post.

"This is Horned Owl," the first Elder said of the man who now approached the fire ring. "He is our eyes and ears in the camp of the wôpusuwak[209]. He is not what he appears to be among the wôpusuwak. Because they think he is unable to hear or see from the haze of their fire water, Horned Owl learns much. The information he brings us is most important and must continue to flow. You must keep this secret for the sake of all our people."

Wôquhsak was stunned by the words of the Elder. Horned Owl stood erect behind the Elder. He looked nothing like the wretch Wôquhsak had seen at the trading post. His clothes were still ragged so he might play the character at the trading post, but all traces of the cowering drunk were missing.

"What you have done, Wôquhsak, is a very brave thing," Horned Owl spoke, his voice firm and steady. "You must know your plan has succeeded. Devon is in chains whimpering and laughing as a madman. They are waiting to take him to the big town across the water to judge him for his crime. You have done well."

Wôquhsak was embarrassed at the praise being given him in the presence of the clan Elders.

"But now, you must not acknowledge me if we meet at the trading posts," Horned Owl continued. "You must let me play my role as you saw me before. Do not show me kindness or acknowledge me in any way. It could endanger our knowing what the wôpusuwak are doing, And, it could put me in danger."

---

[209] White Men

Wôquhsak nodded his understanding and agreement, assured the Elders, and Horned Owl he would never reveal the secret he now knew, not even to Mushqeenupeeash.

"Do you know when Devon is to be moved?" Wôquhsak asked Horned Owl.

"They have sent word across the bay for people to come for him in two-days' time," Horned Owl replied.

Although Wôquhsak said nothing more, he was not yet finished with Devil Devon.

As Wôquhsak walked back to his lodge, he was reflecting on what he had just heard when Mushqeenupeeash hobbled up to him using a long branch from a tree as a kind of cane.

"What did the kuhchâyak[210] want you for?" he asked Wôquhsak anxiously. The question startled Wôquhsak from his thoughts. He knew he could not tell his cousin the full reason for his meeting.

"They had heard Devil Devon has been taken by the wôpusuwak[211]," Wôquhsak said softly. "He is being taken across the pootupâq[212] in two days," he continued beginning to think about something beyond having succeeded.

"You have won, Wôquhsak!" Mushqeenupeeash said with excitement in his voice.

"Not yet," Wôquhsak muttered deep in thought, "the Devil needs to know who has haunted him."

---

[210] Elders
[211] White Men
[212] Narragansett Bay

TWENTY

WÔQUHSAK WALKED WITH A SLOW DETERMINED STEP still deep in thought while Mushqeenupeeash did his best to keep up leaning heavily on his tree branch as a kind of crutch. How was he going to make it clear to Devil Davon that it was these ignorant savages who had unbalanced his mind?

The wôpusuwak[213] had taken the hat and cloak of Jules de Vendome and the war club used to kill him with them when they had bound Devon on the Pequot Trail. Wôquhsak had thought these could be displayed in some way as Devon was taken to the wôpusuwak[214] settlement on the far side of the bay to let him know that his own fears had betrayed him, and it was the ununuwak[215] who had made him feel those fears. Those he saw as inferior had risen against him and won in the name of their friend Jules de Vendome. What could Wôquhsak devise so Devon would know who was responsible for driving him to confess?

Mushqeenupeeash limped along beside his cousin not wanting to disturb him. He was not sure what Wôquhsak was thinking about, but he could see the effort he was putting forth. As he attempted to keep

---

[213] White Men
[214] Ibid Footnote 1
[215] The Narragansett people

pace with him Mushqeenupeeash tripped on a tree root that crossed their path and went down hard, landing on his left side opposite his wound.

The sound of his fall and his cry of pain snapped Wôquhsak out of his thoughts, and he leaned down to help Mushqeenupeeash to his feet.

"I am sorry, natôquhs[216]," Wôquhsak spoke with great feeling. "I was so deep in my mind,,,, I should have kept you from falling."

"You were thinking very hard, natôquhs," Mushqeenupeeash attempted to calm his cousin's concern. "I am not injured, but can I help with what you are thinking about?"

"I want Devon to know who is responsible for his confessing to his crime," Wôquhsak said quietly as he placed the tree branch crutch back in Mushqeenupeeash hand.

"Why is that important?" Mushqeenupeeash replied. "You achieved what you set out to do, Wôquhsak. He has confessed!"

"But, he has confessed out of fear. Fear of what he could not explain and what he believed was pursuing him," Wôquhsak replied. "I want him to know that it is our cleverness that raised his fear."

"Perhaps we should ask Upeeshâwônkoon what, if anything, we could do," Mushqeenupeeash said as they reached the family lodge.

"My mother is clever," Wôquhsak said, agreeing with Mushqeenupeeash, "but we have so little time before he will be far away."

Wôquhsak helped his cousin into the lodge and helped him sit near the fire. He sat beside him and began thinking again for some way to let Devon know the real reason he had confessed.

"You look troubled, my son," Upeeshâwônkoon said softly to Wôquhsak. "Something is bothering you."

"Noohkâs[217]," Wôquhsak replied, "I know I have succeeded in having Devil Devon confess his crime against our friend Jules. But he did so out of fear of being haunted by what he could not explain, and

---

216 Cousin
217 Mother

he believed it was the ghost of his victim. I want him to know it was not a ghost, but the ununuwak[218] whom he looks down upon. Those he considers ignorant and unable to be clever enough to be the cause of his fear."

Upeeshâwônkoon heard the anger in her son's voice and understood his desire to show Devon that the People were not what he thought.

"I thought we would have the cloak and hat of Jules and the pahqumuhq[219] Devon had used to commit his crime. But the wôpusuwak[220] took them all when they bound Devon and took him to the trading post. My thought was to paddle past him as he was being taken out of the cove with the cloak and hat visible in our canoe and whistling the tune of Jules."

Upeeshâwônkoon watched her son and smoothed his black hair as he shed tears of frustration. She knew this was something he wanted badly.

"My son," she said almost as a question, "if you have none of these things, do you not still have your whistle?"

Samual Wilcox was seated in his rocker at the edge of the trading post porch. His appearance was as disheveled as always. Devon sat on his knees on the ground in front of him, a rope behind his back tied his arms at the elbow, his wrists tied with another rope at his waist. Devon had been brought before Wilcox from where he was being held tied against a roof pole in the storage room of the trading post by two of Wilcox's employees.

---

218 The Narragansett People
219 Narragansett war club. Literally, 'head splitter'
220 White Men

"What was you thinkin'?" Wilcox began his interrogation with a question. "Was you thinkin' at all? An' tryin' to blame on them poor savages? Our customers?"

"I know you all hate me!" Devon spat out at the assembled men with as much venom as he could muster. "But none of you liked him either! He strutted about and acted like he was better than any of us!"

"He was one of us, nevertheless," Sam Wilcox intoned. "You killed one of your own," he continued with ice in his voice.

"Yes, it's true! I killed him! I wanted the land that should have been mine!" Devon responded hotly. "You didn't know that, did ye? None of ye did!" Devon was almost screaming. "I lost it to him. I lost it to him on a wager. He cheated: I know he cheated me. He was always lucky."

Sam Wilcox and the other men around him began talking quietly among themselves.

"We know of no wager between you and Jules," Sam responded.

"It was before he came here," Devon replied in disgust. "In fact, he came to claim his prize and rub it in my face. And you all took to him and so did those savages. He strolled about with that tune he whistled like he was such a gentleman."

"Still, he was one of us and you sent the wrong message to the native population here abouts." Sam responded to the approval of those around him. "Look about you. What do you see?"

Devon turned his head in all directions and looked back at his inquisitor with an expression of confusion.

"There is no one here trading," Wilcox intoned. "Our customers have not been here in two days. Not one. That is on you, Devon."

TWENTY-ONE

HIGH WINDS AND ROUGH WATER DELAYED THE ARRIVAL of the shallop from across the great bay to transport Devon to whatever fate awaited him in the wôpusuwak's [221] settlement. Two more days passed before the boat arrived at the trading post in Mill Cove. It's arrival had been seen by scouts of the Narragansett clans stationed at high points along the west edge of the bay.

After unloading the cargo of goods that had been ordered for trade by Wilcox, the captain of the shallop was ready to sail. But because it was late in the day, he decided to layover at the trading post for the night. What did another night matter? Besides, a few more companions at the trading post might not be a bad thing to have with tensions raised among the populace.

As the sun rose in a cloudless sky the next morning, The shallop prepared to sail back across the bay to Newport. Devon was brought from the storeroom still bound as before. Two men, one under each arm, roughly urged him to the wharf where the shallop was tied up. They handed him over to two of the crew who quickly tied his feet with a length of rope as they settled him in the stern of the boat.

---

[221] White Men's

140

_____><_____

Wôquhsak's people were aware of every movement taking place at the trading posts from the time the sail was spotted in the bay approaching the cove. People had been watching the activity at the trading post from across the cove and sending reports back to the clan's summer camp. Runners from their camp had carried the news of what had happened, and was happening, to every clan along the shore. They also carried a message from Wôquhsak and the Elders of his clan: be prepared to carry out Wôquhsak's plan. Each runner had received instructions to be relayed to the Elders of every clan.

At first light on the third day after the sail had been sighted approaching the west shore of the bay, word came from the cove watchers that the boat was preparing to leave. As soon as word was received, Wôquhsak sent runners to the other clans along the shore. It was time. Everyone from Wôquhsak's clan who could walk, and from every clan along the shore within distance, began to assemble. Only the sick and elderly stayed behind.

A few strokes of the paddles kept aboard the boat moved it away from the wharf at the trading post and turned it, so it was headed into the wind. The sail was raised and luffed in the light breeze until it filled and was trimmed by the crew. Because the wind was light in the cove and from the southwest coming over the land, it took a while to reach any speed. As the boat rounded the island in the cove and headed for its inlet, something could begin to be seen in the distance.

As the shallop reached the spit of land that marked the exit from the cove, assembled on the sand were several dozen Narragansett clans, nearly a hundred in number. They stood watching as the shallop approached them. The crew of the shallop looked on in silence. Devon raised his head to see what had attracted the crew's attention. As they drew nearer, the crew could hear something. The assembled group was whistling. They were whistling not randomly, but a melody. It was Jules de Vendome's tune.

Devon began to laugh quietly. The laughter then grew until it was a wild, insane, evil cackle of a man gone mad. As the boat tacked out into the bay, the sound of the whistling faded. But the sound of insane laughter continued to be carried on the wind from the crazed man in the sailboat.

ABOUT THE AUTHOR

ROBERT BAILEY STONE has written two previous books: *The Chronicles of Benjamin Prescott*, a work of historical fiction, and *Murder in Rock Cove*, a murder/mystery. He is originally from Long Island, New York and has resided in Rhode Island since 1985. He is a graduate of Union College in Schenectady, N.Y. with a Bachelor of Science degree in Geology. Mr. Stone has a background in financial services business and now writes as a second career. He has been married to his spouse Angela for fifty-five years and has two sons and three grandchildren.

Follow the author's Facebook page: *RBS Books*

www.ingramcontent.com/pod-product-compliance
Lightning Source LLC
Chambersburg PA
CBHW060648260626
47161CB00008B/3057